This book is dedicated to my Mom, Christina, my Dad, John, my sister Hannah and my brother, Jacob who have supported me in my writing efforts and have helped me become the person that I am.

CONTENTS

Hillgregg
The Temple of Thought

Prologue

The story takes place in a land called Voulkar. Voulkar is a world parallel to ours in a different dimension of space and time. It's a place dominated by nature and wildlife except for a small nation known as Naxece. By 1583, it was mainly controlled by three economic powers: the village of Hillgregg, mostly inhabited by humans, the village of Mondas, also ruled by humans, and the web-like village of Alknarav, run by a race of large spiders simply called Arachnids. Other regions included the Hillland, dominated by the nomadic People of the Hill, the Trees, controlled by the Tree People, the gardens, a province owned by Hillgregg, the Cliffs, run by the Cliff People, and the Thickets, an uninhabited forest that is to this day seen as hostile (and for good reason).

But in 1624, an aggressive Arachnid named Akkrawn took control over all of Alknarav, and in 1626, declared war on the rest of Naxece. His troops headed quickly for Mondas, and, after a long, hard-fought battle, the Arachnids destroyed it, creating what is today called The Mondas Battlefield. But Akkrawn was a fool. For some reason, he never let his army leave the ruined Mondas. Hillgregg troops, with the help of their fiercely loyal ally, the Cliff People, surrounded and annihilated the arachnid forces. They then attacked and destroyed Alknarav, and murdered Akkrawn. Although the war ended less than a year after it had started, two of the greatest villages in Naxece were destroyed by it. The Arachnids are said to be extinct today, but some whispers cannot be silenced...

In the Beginning

Chapter 1

A man trekked through an immense desert, as the wind moaned through the bleak, grey sky around him. Never before had one seen such an unimaginably hellish environment, yet it was not the only one this man knew.

He approached the entrance to a cave, which was guarded by a hulking being.

"I am Forlex," said the man, "Allow me entrance."

The creature moved aside, and Forlex began to move deep into the cave.

He eventually came to a man in a chair, guarded by the giant beasts, and draped in shadowy darkness. "Forlex," he said, in a hushed whisper, "Why have you summoned me here?"

"I have news, my king," said Forlex. "There has been a birth."

"Of what relevance is this?" said the other man.

"One of the powers," said Forlex.

"Oh, my," said the other man, still in a whisper, "Are you sure of this?"

"Yes," said Forlex, "The Beylphegans have confirmed it."

"That is very disturbing indeed," said the other man.

"Shall I make preparations?" asked Forlex.

"No," said the man. "We must wait. However, do inform me of any other relevant births."

"Yes, sir," said Forlex.

Over the course of the year, two more births occurred, and finally, one more.

"My lord, we must take action," said Forlex.

"No," said the man, "we are not yet even sure that the legends are true. We must not reveal ourselves until we are absolutely certain."

"So what shall we do for now?" asked Forlex anxiously.

"We wait," said the shadowy man.

23 Years Later

Chapter 2

In Hillgregg there was a man named Rike Pathis, and all he could do was run. He could hear the beast coming closer and closer as he attempted to flee from it. As he reached the edge of a cliff, he was able to turn around quickly and see the creature running at him. It was at least thirty feet tall, and appeared to be made out of bones and corpses, all mutilated and twisted together in one, hideous figure. The monster got right in his face and began screeching loudly. *Funny,* he thought, *that sounds kind of like...*

... My alarm clock, great, Rike thought, fumbling around his clock attempting to silence the annoying sound. When he finally succeeded, he gathered his wits, took a shower, threw on some clothes, grabbed a nut bar, and left.

Since the War of the Arachnids, Hillgregg had become as complex and intricate as Naxece itself had once been. Hillgregg was divided into six main sections: Uppergregg, Midgregg, Undergregg, Outergregg, Hillgregg Prison, and the Industrial Park. While

23 Years Later

Hillgregg had no official leader, there was a city council that made all the major decisions.

Rike lived in a small apartment in Undergregg, and he worked as a crystal harvester throughout the city. His job was among the most important in Hillgregg, as crystal infestations often became potentially dangerous, and crystals were one of the city's most valuable resources. However, crystal harvesters were poorly paid and often took a backseat to the sculptors and craftsmen, and other who made use of the crystals they harvested. Rike was 23, well built, had short, brown hair, and worked with three others who were the same age as him, and also, like Rike, couldn't afford college.

As Rike arrived at his office, he met up with two of his co-workers, Krilden Serthik (often called 'Krill,' because of his small size) and Adria Varsus. Krill had jet-black short hair, which laid flat against his head, almost as if it had been painted on. While he was short, and not particularly muscular, he made up for it with his cunning intelligence. The main reason he didn't receive a scholarship was because Krill was incredibly lazy throughout high school. He never forgave himself for that, so he devoted himself to studies.

Adria was a thin, strong, and, often times aggressive young woman. She had long, dark brown hair, and had calm, but penetrating eyes, almost as if she could see into a person's soul (as if she wasn't intimidating enough already). She, unlike Krill, was perfectly fine, not getting into college. However, her parents weren't. She always resented them for that.

"So do we have any jobs today yet?" Rike asked. "Well, no, not yet," said Adria. "Anyway," she added, "We're one short." "Jirkir's late again, I take it?" Rike said, noticing his friend's absence. "I'll call him, because even though this is fifth time he's late this month, we wouldn't be able to eat if it weren't for The Jerker." Jirkir Karver was known for being incredibly irresponsible, lazy, and often times, drunk, but he got his nickname, 'The Jerker' because of his ability to pull crystals from their foundations in a single jerk. He had messy brown hair, had a hint of a beard, and frequently would show up to work with bloodshot eyes, as a result of the previous night's activities.

Rike pulled out his cell phone and dialed Jirkir's number.

"Hullo?" Jirkir mumbled through the phone.

"Hey, Jirkir, it's Rike, how drunk were you last night?" he asked.

"I wuh no drun," Jirkir muttered in reply.

"Yeah whatever, just get down here whenever your hangover ends," Rike said, hanging up the phone. "Well, judging by how sick he sounded, we've got at least a couple hours until he gets here, so for right now, let's just do what we can here at the office." Rike announced.

"Uh, I'll go see if anyone's called us with a job," Krill said.

After he went inside, Adria looked at Rike with a concerned face. "What?" Rike asked.

"Oh, you know!" Adria exclaimed. "Jirkir is such a bum!"

"Oh, come on," Rike pleaded, "He's still not happy about how his life is turning out."

23 Years Later

"So?" Adria shouted, "That ship sailed four years ago, and in case you haven't noticed, you, me, and Krill couldn't afford college either, but none of us drown our sorrows in a million gallons of beer!" "Hey!" Rike yelled, "If you think Jirkir being late all the time doesn't piss me off too, it does. But he's been my best friend for years, and as I've said before, our business wouldn't survive without him. You understand that, don't you?"

"Yeah, I guess," Adria murmured. "I just wish he would act a little more mature."

"Hey, he'll come around, trust me," Rike reassured. "But until then, we'll just have to work with him as he is."

"Okay," Adria said with a sigh. "Oh, we'd better head in and see if Krill's gotten any calls about jobs."

They both walked inside, and when they approached Krill at the phone desk. "So who blew up first?" he asked.

"Shut up, Krill!" Adria snapped.

"Well, I'm just saying, you guys have this same stupid fight every time that dumbell's late for work," Krill explained.

"Anyway, it was Adria," Rike muttered under his breath. Adria heard him, and she punched him in the stomach.
"Ow! Good Lord, Adria, I was only kidding!" he said.

As things were starting to heat up again, Jirkir walked in. "Hey, did I already miss the eruption?" he asked jokingly.
"JIRKIR, YOU LITTLE- well, actually, yeah, you did," Rike admitted with a chuckle.
"That was fast," Adria said in a surprised voice, "When Rike called, you were so hung over that I could barely understand what you were saying."
Jirkir smiled and said, "Yeah, well a little after that I puked for about fifteen seconds straight, and I felt much better."
"How'd you get here so fast?" asked Adria inquisitively.
"When I woke up, I was still parked by the bar about a block from here," he said with a half-smile.
"I should have guessed," Adria sneered.

"Whatever, Krill, do we have any jobs?" Rike questioned. Right after he asked the phone began to ring.
"Why, yes, I believe we do," Krill said sarcastically. He quickly picked up the

phone. "Sharp Point Harvesters, this is Krilden, how may I help you? Really? Right now? Okay, we'll be right there." Krill hung up the phone. "Gear up, guys," he said, "We're headed for Outergregg, there's a crystal infestation in the Hot Springs."

"Off to the Jerk-Mobile," Jirkir announced. "Will you stop calling it that?" Adria pleaded, "We all pitched in to buy that van, and you know it!"

"Yeah, but I pitched in a dollar more than everybody else," Jirkir boasted.

"No, you pitched in a dollar *less* than everybody else," Krill corrected.

"Come on, Rike, back me up," Jirkir said.

"Sorry man, not gonna back you up there," said Rike.

As they boarded their less-than-state of the art van, Rike struggled to get the old V4 engine running. *Come on, live,* he thought. As the vehicle hummed to life, Rike stepped on the gas, and took it to the road. "Why do we drive around in this piece of crap?" Jirkir wondered.

"You were the one calling it 'the Jirk-Mobile'," Rike argued.

"I know," Jirkir said, "but it might as well be brown and have flies swarming around it."

As they exited the business section of Undergregg, they passed through Central Undergregg, home to Hillgregg's working class. There might as well have been a crack in the concrete for every broken dream that resided there. Undergregg was also the unofficial crime capital of Hillgregg, mainly thanks to the city's resident mob superpower, the Legion. However, Undergregg wasn't all that bad. It was, in every way, the foundation of Hillgregg. Not only was it the physical foundation, but also those who resided there supported the rest of Hillgregg and greatly contributed to the city's thriving economy, especially the crystal harvesters who provided Hillgregg's most valuable export.

"Ladies and gentlemen, we are nearing Undergregg Tunnel," Rike announced. Undergregg Tunnel was the only highway in and out of Undergregg. It was also known for being remarkably clean, the road practically being a reflective surface. This was mainly because all cars in Hillgregg hovered, so there were no tire marks, but partly because every day the tunnel's streets were covered in a layer of mutated parasites, which could decompose any form of litter in seconds.

"Ah, natural light," Jirkir said as they exited into Midgregg.
"Hey guys," Rike asked, "what's the fastest way to Outergregg? We don't exactly have a lot of gas here." "I think the shortest way is through the Grand Market," Adria said. The Grand Market was *the* place in Hillgregg for food and other necessities. "Okay, the Grand Market it is," Rike said.

Elsewhere, something dark was unfolding. "Life signs are still negative," said Doctor Soller. "Pump in some more crystals, I want that corpse completely filled," Doctor Klise ordered.
"Yes, doctor," Doctor Soller said nervously. He pulled a switch and more and more crystals were pushed into the body until it was, as Dr. Klise wanted it, completely filled. Dr. Soller then looked at his computer and said, "Life signs are still- Wait! There's a small sign of life, and it's growing by the second!" "Good," said Dr. Klise with a smile, "now marks

the beginning of something great." As the life signs continued to skyrocket, the creature began to stir...

Crystal Harvesting

Chapter 3

Jirkir spat when he saw the entrance sign to the Hillgregg Hot Springs:

Hillgregg Hot Springs
Built on the remains of the 51st Parallel
"Well, guys, welcome to resort de la people who have a ridiculously large amount of money," Jirkir sneered as the crew entered the premises. Even though it was typical of Jirkir to poke fun at Hillgregg's richest, this time he was actually right. The Hillgregg Hot Springs required so many payments and fees that you'd be up to your eyeballs in debt unless you had about a million expendable dollars. To Jirkir, this was the greatest example of how condescending rich people could be.
Krill then optimistically said, "Hey, at least we'll get to get a good long look at it while we're harvesting."
"Thank you!" Rike said, patting Krill on the back, "That's the kind of attitude we

need," he said, scowling at Jirkir jokingly.

"What's the 51st Parallel anyway?" Jirkir asked. Krill sighed, as if annoyed having to explain it.

"The 51st Parallel," he said, "was the imaginary line that separated Hillgregg during the Hillgregg Civil War, and I guess this is the exact location of the 51st Parallel."

"Fitting," Jirkir said, "these guys try to make themselves important as possible."

As they approached the main gatekeeper, he gave them a disgusted look. "May I help you?" the man asked with a snarl.

"See what I mean?" Jirkir whispered to Adria.

"Uh, yeah," Rike said to the gatekeeper, "We're the crystal harvesters."

"Oh, yes, *you*," the gatekeeper said in an annoyed tone. "You're expected in the Undercaves, a little to the right."

"Um, thanks," Rike said.

As soon as they were out of the gatekeeper's earshot, Jirkir began talking angrily. "Well, you were right, Krill, we'll get to take a good, long, look at how the other half lives as we clean out their boiler room!" Adria, clearly frustrated as well, then added sarcastically, "Well at least that guy only *implied* that we're garbage, and didn't actually *say* it."

"Come on, guys," Rike said, "We've got to stay positive. Just because one guy here is a total jerk doesn't mean that everybody here is. He's probably just used to seeing people who well- aren't us," he said while trying to hold back laughter.

Soon they approached a small door on the side of the entrance marked 'Undercaves.' "This must be it," Krill said.

"Really?" Jirkir asked grouchily, "What was your first clue, that it says 'Undercaves', or the fact that it's the only pathetic-looking door on this whole resort?"

"Uh – I – uh, the first one, I guess," Krill stuttered.

"Down, boy," Rike said to Jirkir. "We have to keep our heads if we ever want to get hired here again."

"What makes you think I want to?" Jirkir questioned.

"Majority rules," Rike answered.

"Crap," Jirkir said, "I hate it when you do that."

Crystal Harvesting

As they entered the door, a man, who was dressed in an expensive suit, greeted Rike. "Ah, you must be Rike," the man said, shaking his hand. "Uh, yes," Rike said "and this is Jirkir, Adria, and Krilden. We are Sharp Point Harvesters."

"My name is Plazer Thernsten," the man said, "owner and general manager of the Hillgregg Hot Springs. It's mighty fortunate of you to come on such short notice. This heavy infestation is already starting to take a toll on our profits. You see, the Undercaves are where all our pumps, heaters, and generators are down there, and with that area clogged up, the Hot Springs have no power."

"We understand the level of importance, but, uh, where are the caves?" Adria asked (noticing the room they were in did not appear cave-like at all). "Oh, but of course," said Plazer, "This is just the main entryway. The Undercaves are just down that elevator," he said, pointing to a set of metal doors at the end of the room. "Just come back and tell me when you're done."

"Okay, good deal," Rike said. The team then got into the elevator and slowly began descending.

"Okay, that guy cannot be rich," exclaimed Jirkir, "He was way too nice."

"Well, Jirkir, it *is* possible for rich people to be nice, despite how shocking it is," said Adria, rolling her eyes at him.

"Alright, cut the crap guys, and let's focus on getting this job done," Rike announced. The doors opened, and they exited the elevator.

"Wow, this really must be where the Hot Springs get their HOT," said Krill. You could tell the Undercaves were hot before you felt it. The walls of the caves themselves seemed to sweat with their shining humidity.

"Well, let's hurry up so we can get out of here," said Jirkir, already panting.

"Come on, quit being a baby," said Rike.

I must find it. That was the only thing running through his head. *I must find it, I must find it, I must find it!* He just kept thinking that as he continued to speed toward his destination at an astonishing rate. *I must find it, I will find it! The fate of my people and their future is in my hands.*

The team harvested crystals slowly, but surely by sucking their roots out into their telepacks (except for Jirkir, who jerked the living rocks out and threw them into the telepack). Crystals were immortal, and couldn't be killed by being harvested or sculpted, so they always retained their beautiful glow. The function of a telepack was to teleport the crystals to the vault back at the group's office immediately after they reached the inside of the bag.

As they reached a dimly lit area where crystals were clearly absent, the ground began to shake slightly.
"Uh, guys, are you completely ignoring the fact that the very ground beneath our feet is quaking?" Jirkir said nervously.
"Relax, idiot," Adria said, "we've just come across some seismium water heaters." Seismium was a unique element that, when exposed to solid matter, caused it to shake. However, when in contact with liquid matter, seismium caused it to heat up.

"Well, wait a minute, then why aren't there any crystals in here?" Jirkir asked wonderingly. "Simple," Krill said, "the ground is moving too much for a crystal's roots to set in."

"So, if this stuff causes quakes, couldn't you use it as a weapon?" Jirkir questioned.

"Yeah, but it's too unstable. If you just shot a bunch of seismium into the ground during battle, you could end up hurting both sides of whatever war you're fighting," Krill responded.

"Wow, Krill," said Jirkir, "not bad for a guy whose head only reaches my neck."

"Well, there are some advantages to that," Krill said with a smile, "it's easier to do this." He then proceeded to punch Jirkir in the, well, you know where.

"Aaauugghh," Jirkir moaned. "Yeah, I'd call that an advantage." Krill was okay with his nickname, but making fun of his height otherwise wasn't a smart thing to do, so the others usually kept quiet about it. They only did when they were feeling really brave, lucky, or, in some cases with Jirkir, really, really, really, really wasted.

"Okay, it looks like we're back in our jurisdiction," Rike said, noticing that the ground was no longer shaking and crystals were reappearing. "Back to work, guys- Jirkir, get up!"

"Hey," Jirkir said with a groan, "why wouldn't you be doing this too if you'd just been hit in the crotch?"

"Because, Jirkir," Rike responded, "I'm not a pussy, like you."

The rest of the job was uneventful, yet it went by pretty fast. All they did was sweep through one more tunnel and then headed back to the elevator. Plazer was there to greet them. "Did everything go okay without a hitch?" he asked them.

"Yeah, I guess," Rike said. "Except one of us got spooked by a few seismium heaters," Krill said, turning his eyes toward Jirkir.

"Here," said Plazer, handing each of them a thick wad of cash, "This is nowhere near what I owe you. Your van is in our garage, right around the corner."

"Why is it in-,"

"Thank you for your help," said Plazer, cutting off Rike.

"Um, your welcome," Rike said. They then left and headed for the garage.

"Okay, I'd say again that he's too nice to be rich, but if he was, then I wouldn't have all this money," Jirkir said, smiling.

"Here's the garage," Rike said.
"Hey guys, check this out," said Adria, looking at a piece of paper taped to the garage door. What it said was:

I hope this covers everything I owe you. Take a look at your new transport.

-Plazer

Rike opened the garage door and saw what the note meant. In the garage was a sleek, long, blue and silver car.
"It's a Ride Chaser," Jirkir said, barely able to get the words out.
"Well, let's stop staring at it and actually drive it," Rike said.

The interior was even better than the outside. The seats were leather, there was non-stop AC, and the seats reclined too.
"Well, let's see how fast this thing can go," Rike said, turning the key. The engine quietly turned on, and Rike drove the car off with smooth speed.

When they arrived back at their office, Jirkir got out of the car and said, "Best...job...ever." "Okay, happy face,"

Crystal Harvesting

Krill said, "Glad you're in a good mood, because the day's not over yet. I'm gonna go check the phone and see if any more work has come our way." He headed in, coming out a short time later. "We got a call at eleven," Krill said, "about an infestation at the Silver Towers."

"Really? That's unusual," said Adria, "Crystal harvesters rarely ever get jobs outside of Hillgregg." "Well, we just did," Rike said, "so let's pile back into that nice new car and get going."

The Silver Towers were located at the bottom of the hillland, and they were an area dedicated to scientific research and experimentation. An infestation there was unusual, but they did happen, and at this moment, fate sent the Sharp Point Harvesters there to clean up.

As they crossed through the hillland and neared the Silver Towers, the team began to notice something. "Dear God," Adria said in astonishment. "What are you- holy crap," Rike said. "What's everybody- oh my God," Krill said.

"Hey, why's everybody stopping in mid-sen- whoa," said Jirkir.

Chapter 4

The Silver Towers were in ruins. One of them was completely burned down, and the rest were really beat up. "Hang on, guys," Rike said, "I'm gonna get in closer to see if we can't figure out what happened here."

"Whatever it is, it probably doesn't involve us," Jirkir said.

"Oh, come on Jirkir," Rike said, "haven't you ever wanted to go right into the belly of the beast?" "No," Jirkir said. "Oh, well, you're going anyway," said Rike.

After parking their car near the entrance to the Towers, the team approached a directory map of the premises. "Well, now I can see why only one building burned down," said Krill, observing the map. "The building that was destroyed was the explosives test facility. Somehow, up to a few of the bombs went off, which triggered every explosive in the building to detonate. The chemical bombs must have had enough force to kill everyone in the Silver Towers."

"Then why aren't we dying?" asked Adria. "These were only small chemical bombs," Krill said. "The toxic gases probably dissipated after a short while. The bigger nukes are built, tested, and tampered with at Area UG-28 back in Undergregg."

"Alright, clearly we can't get any evidence from the explosives facility, so what's the tower nearest to that one?" Rike asked.

"Uh, let's see," said Krill, "it looks like that would be the genetics facility."

"And where was the crystal infestation reported to be?" Rike asked.

"The message said it was in the," Krill paused for a moment. "The genetics facility."

"Okay, then that's where we're headed," Rike announced. "Come on, guys," he said.

"I'd say it's your funeral," Jirkir mumbled, "but I'm going with you."

As they walked through the Silver Towers, the evidence of destruction became even more prevalent. Sparks flew from the power lines, and broken glass littered the ground.

"Alright, people," said Rike, "any theories?" "Could be the Crystal Ball Syndicate," Adria said. "Nah," Jirkir replied, "those jerk-offs are more of a cross if crossed gang, and I doubt they considered a bunch of nerdy science geeks a threat."

"Hey," Krill said, "those 'nerdy science geeks' gave us some of the greatest technology ever invented, ever since this place was founded in 1955."

"Ugghh," Jirkir groaned, "you sound just like my high school history book, and in fact, the only difference is I can't figure out how to shut you up!"

"Cut the crap, you two!" Rike yelled. "Anyway, I think we're here."

The Genetics Tower was a bit more scuffed up than the surrounding facilities, so it was clear that whatever happened started in there. "Okay, I'm guessing this is the part where we call the cops, and then they take care of everything?" Jirkir said.

"No," Rike said, "this is the part where you shut the flip up and we all go inside the building." "But-," Jirkir said before he was cut off by Krill racking

him again. "Owww! What was that for?"
Jirkir asked.
"For not shutting the flip up," Krill
answered.

When they entered the Genetics
building, Krill immediately approached a
large screen with a keyboard in front of
it. "Hmm," he said, turning it on,
"fortunately the filing computer seems
intact." "Okay," Rike said, "whatever
went down most likely happened after
we were called in, so let's check the files
from after eleven."
"Alright," Krill responded, opening up
the files. "Huh," he said, it seems two
scientists, Doctors Klise and Soller, were
reported missing at 11:10 this morning,
but it looks like we've got bigger fish to
fry. It says we triggered an intruder
alarm at 10:00 am, and that we went into
this building at 12:00 am."
"So, what does that mean, we're being
framed?" asked Adria.
"I don't think intentionally," said Krill,
"the explosion must have somehow
messed up the clocks around here."
"Either way," said Jirkir, "We're screwed."

"Okay, so how long does it normally take to seal off a crystal-infested area?" Rike asked.

"Around ten minutes," Krill answered.

"So, knowing that, we can guess that the two missing doctors were sealed inside the infested zone, and something went wrong in there," Rike said. "Krill, where's the infestation?" he asked.

"Uh," Krill said, searching through some files, "that would be the Upper Wing, specifically the top floor of the tower."

"Okay, let's head to the elevator," Jirkir announced.

"Uh, yeah, about that," Krill said, "the elevator could have been damaged."

"Oh, good lord, please, no," said Jirkir.

Once they had climbed all the stairs, Jirkir immediately collapsed. "My legs! My arms! My whole body!"

"Just ignore him," Rike whispered to Adria. "He'll most likely get right up once he realizes he's not getting any attention."

"Alright, so this is the infested zone. Now let's head in and see what went on," Rike said.

The room they entered was full of crystals, but they also noticed a table with bizarre injector-like devices hovering over it. "Hey guys," Krill said sitting at a computer, "We lucked out. Looks like this computer is untouched. I'm gonna take a look at the logs."

ENTRY 256907

TODAY IS THE DAY THAT PROJECT CARVANER WILL SUCCEED AT LAST. THE CORPSE DOCTOR SOLLER AND I FOUND AT THE ARACHNID WARGRAVES IS A PERFECT SPECIMEN FOR THIS EXPERIMENT. CRYSTALS WILL BE ABLE TO MOVE FREELY IN THEIR OWN BODIES. AT THE MOMENT, WE ARE THE ONLY TWO SCIENTISTS IN THE SILVER TOWERS WHO ARE AWARE OF THE EXISTENCE OF THIS PROJECT. SO, TO KEEP IT UNDER WRAPS, DOCTOR SOLLER AND I HAVE DECIDED TO PERFORM THE TEST IN A SEALED AREA INFESTED WITH CRYSTALS. THE FIRST INJECTIONS ARE NOW TAKING PLACE. LIFE SIGNS READ NEGATIVE. SECOND INJECTIONS NOW UNDERWAY. LIFE SIGNS ARE POSITIVE, AND ARE RISING BY THE

"That's all there is left," Krill said. They all stood in silence for a moment.

"Okay," Jirkir finally said, "what part of bringing an extinct evil warrior to life sounded like a good idea to these guys?"

"Well," Krill said, "they probably thought the crystal mind would be dominant, but apparently that theory was proven false. But what I'm really wondering is where this thing went."

"Hey, guys," exclaimed Jirkir, "I found a security camera."

"Well, let's have a look," said Rike inquisitively.

Jirkir took the tape out of the camera, which appeared to have a bullet hole in it, and pushed the security tape into a nearby monitor. The first thing that appeared on the screen was static, which triggered deep anticipation among the group. "This isn't helping," sighed Jirkir, reaching for the monitor.

Just as he said this, an image appeared on the screen. Two men were doing what looked like average busywork. Then, all of the sudden, a loud bang was heard, presumably the door slamming open. There were two gunshots, and in an instant, the two men were dead, and a familiar voice began shouting out orders.

"Clear all the files!," yelled Rike on-screen. Krill, Jirkir, Adria, and he were all wearing biohazard suits. Krill walked over to the computer and typed something in. It'll take a bit, but they'll be gone before anyone's found them."

The real Krill suddenly swerved over to the computer. "Hang on," he said, "I'll see if I can figure this out." Back on screen, Jirkir could be seen creating a mobile zip line (with a bomb attached to it) to the Explosives Tower. "Come on," said on-screen Rike, "let's get out of here before it detonates." "Hold on," said on-screen Adria, who then shot the camera. Then there was only static.

"Well, so much for Krill's 'unintentional' theory," said Jirkir.

"How are those files coming?" Rike asked nervously.

"Whatever virus was installed has run its course," murmured Krill, dazed. "The files are gone."

"So what do we do now?" asked Adria.

"I think we should start at the Arachnid wargraves," Rike said.

Krill was the first to respond. "Rike, the only known Arachnid wargraves are located in the heart of the Thickets."

"Yeah," Adria added, "and I have no desire to see what's in there."

"For the record, I didn't even want to come in here," said Jirkir.

"Can't your dad help us out?" asked Jirkir.

"No," sighed Rike, "Look at all we've got on us. With his help, we'll be lucky not to get the death penalty."

"I guess we've got no other options," said Adria.

"Besides, I've always been a bit curious about what's in there," said Krill. "Well, right now, I could either die in prison or in the Thickets, so I guess it doesn't really matter," said Jirkir.

"Great," said Rike, "then we're all in agreement. Now let's hurry up and leave, before the police come for us."

Slogs and Secrets

Chapter 5

The ride to the thickets was long and quiet. When they finally arrived, Jirkir was the first one to speak. "Welcome to Hell, my friends," he said.   "Okay, so, we're looking for the Arachnid wargraves," said Rike, "Where are they?" he asked, looking at Krill.

"If I have my history right," Krill said, "than the wargraves are in the same location as the Arachnid war base, and that would be near the center of the Thickets."

"How convenient," Adria said sarcastically. "Well, that was actually the intention of the Arachnids during the war," Krill said. "They wanted to be completely surrounded by the Thickets so they'd be almost completely invulnerable to Mondas' troops and attacks."

"Enough talk," Rike said, "the sooner we go in the sooner we can get this over with."

The second they entered the Thickets, the team could immediately feel a sense of danger from everything they saw.

Slogs and Secrets

"I'm tired," said Jirkir, panting, "hey, let's go rest in this cave," he said, pointing to an opening in a nearby wall of rock.
"Jirkir, YOU IDIOT!" said Krill. "Take a closer look at that cave!" Jirkir squinted at the cave and noticed orange worms crawling around it.

"Those bugs are boarnoit worms," Krill said. "They enter the body through any opening they can find, and then they eat your inner organs, and once they're done with you, you might as well be a bear skin rug."

"I'll keep that in mind- shorty," said Jirkir. Krill then racked him.
"You know, after I've already done that twice, I at least expected you to cover yourself," said Krill. "What a butthead," Jirkir muttered.

As they continued to trudge through the thick mud, the Thickets grew steadily darker. The plants seemed to be staring back at them (and sometimes they actually were).

At one point the team reached a funny-looking tree, which Krill warned them not to go near. "That's a slog tree," he said. "Those holes in the branches ooze out green slogs, which engulf their victims and melt them into food matter from the outside in, and they grow as much as the size of whatever they eat."

There was only one instance on the journey when anyone was actually attacked. "What's that doing there?" Adria asked, pointing to a large tree root. "It's a tree root, what's the problem?" said Rike. "There's no tree," said Krill, noticing that there was, indeed, no tree was close enough to the root for it to be that large.

Suddenly, part of the root pulled out of the ground to reveal a large pointed spike at the end of it. It then jabbed at Adria, who was pushed out of the way by Rike. "Thanks," said Adria. "No problem," said Rike.

"Aw, crap," said Krill, running away from the object. "It's a graller." As everyone attempted to run away, the graller sprouted up taller and stabbed at the ground around it.

As the graller aimed for Rike, Krill shouted something. "Rike, use your crystal sucker, it might be enough to suffocate the beast!" Rike quickly pulled out his telepack (they were portable, so the team carried them everywhere), stuck it to the graller's pointed head, and pressed the suck button.

The graller immediately began flailing around in pain, trying to remove the telepack from itself. After a few seconds, it finally collapsed on the ground with a thud. Rike then removed his telepack. "Let's go," he said.

After about another hour of walking through the treacherous Thickets, the team finally reached a large opening full of broken war machines and small buildings, which were clearly tombs. "Looks like we're here," Jirkir said, "now what are we looking for?"
"I think I know the answer to that," Adria said, looking at a nearby tomb. The rest of the team headed over there and they saw what she meant. There was a single word, written in blood, on the door of the tomb. It was a bit faded, but they could still read it clearly:
CARVANER

"Well, I think we found where the missing corpse came from," said Adria. "Let's see what we can learn inside," Rike said.

Slogs and Secrets

It took some force, but the door came open pretty easily. Inside, there was a trail of blood leading right to a coffin. The lid to the coffin was wide open. There wasn't a body inside, but there was a small notebook. "What have we here?" said Jirkir, opening the book.

April 15, 1626, war journals of General Carvaner of the Arachnid army

We have set up base in the Thickets and are preparing to attack Mondas. Our orders are to rip the village apart until we find the Temple. Akkrawn is convinced it is there, but I still believe that it could be in Hillgregg.

April 19, 1626

Our battle with Mondas was a complete success. Their soldiers were wiped out quickly, and that made terminating the civilian population much easier. We have knocked over and destroyed every building in the village, and we still have not found the Temple. I still have my doubts, but Akkrawn has ordered us to keep searching.

June 3, 1626

Hillgregg troops have eliminated our forces in Mondas, and are closing in on our war base fast. I knew it was in Hillgregg, but now I don't think the Arachnids will ever control what it holds. My body will be buried with this journal, in the very room I am writing in, the room that will become my grave.

July 14, 2009

I have learned this date from one of the humans who revived me before I killed him, along with all of the other humans in that area. Now I finally have the chance to remake the Arachnids. I will return to this place again once I've found the Temple of Thought in Hillgregg.

"What's the Temple of Thought?" Jirkir asked.

"I don't know," said Krill. "Whatever it is, it's back in Hillgregg, and Carvaner's probably already there looking for it."

"I guess we'll just have to beat him to it," said Rike. At this point, everyone else knew it was pointless to argue with him.

When they exited the tomb, there was a giant blob of green slime directly ahead of them, and it was spreading fast.

"I take it that's a slog," said Jirkir.

"Yeah," Krill said, "but I think this one stuffed itself a bit." The one thing about slogs that Krill left out: it had a pair of dark, cold, silvery eyes.

"Run!" Rike yelled. As they began to run, the giant slog started to rush at them faster.

"Over here, guys!" Krill said. "I think I saw an Arachnid deployment ship up ahead. It looked like it might still work!"

The team quickly boarded the deployer ship, and Rike and Krill were

successfully able to get it started.
"Okay, let's get out of here!" said Jirkir.
"Are you kidding?" Krill said, "That thing's way too big for us to escape. We'll have to kill it."
    "WHAT?" Jirkir said.
"Just trust me," Krill said. "Rike, go straight for the slog's head."
"Okay," Rike said unconfidently. They rocketed toward the monster's head at an incredible speed. "Oh, and everybody put a parachute on, you'll need it," Krill said.
    They got within a few feet of the slog's head. "Okay, push the deployment button!" Krill yelled. Rike pushed the button and the bottom of the ship dropped down and they all fell out. Then they stopped falling. There was no parachute above them, but they remained in the air.
"Oh," said Krill, "jetpacks." They all watched as the ship flew right into the creature's head. It then fell to the ground and vanished. "The ship was going fast enough that it was able to go right to the slog's brain, and that killed it."

"You insane creature," Jirkir said, "Let's jetpack to the Ride Chaser. It beats walking," he said.

They returned to the car and all boarded it. "Alright, what's our plan?" Adria asked.

"I'll head to the Uppergregg Museum," Krill said. "Maybe they've heard of this Temple of Thought." "I'll go to the Hillgregg Mines," Jirkir said. "They could have uncovered something."

"I'll go to the Gardenian Caverns," said Adria.

"I'll go to Alknarav," Rike said, "and see if the Arachnids left any clues behind." They fired up the car and left the Thickets.

Holocaust Ruins

Chapter 6

Rike got off the Ride Chaser and observed the rickety Alknarav Staircase. *I guess it's safe,* he thought. He began to climb it, and the first step collapsed beneath him. *Arachnid geriatrics,* he thought as the second stair also collapsed. *Ah, screw it.* He turned on his jetpack and rocketed up to the top. Rike then saw a giant web wall surrounding Alknarav. Akkrawn had it spun to separate the arachnids from what he believed to be their enemies. Fortunately for Rike, however, the attack on Alknarav by Hillgregg and the Cliff People had created large holes in the wall that Rike could easily walk through. It wasn't until then that Rike had a full view of the destroyed village. Some of the buildings were still intact, but there were bones everywhere, and there was an eerie feeling of death in the air.

Well, this should be fun. Not only have I had to keep everyone I work with from killing each other, but now I get to search through every beat-up shack in this ghost town until I find something about the Temple of Thought, whatever the hell that is!

He walked up to the closest building, a small house, and when he turned the knob, the door fell down. He searched the entire house but found nothing of importance. It was the same with the next several buildings.

Aw, crap, what the flip was I thinking? This'll be the death of all of us! We can barely survive a workday together, how can we possibly make it through this? Jirkir and Krill hate each other, Adria hates Jirkir, and they all want me to side with them!

Since he started his job as a crystal harvester, he couldn't help feeling like a parent to his co-workers. Jirkir was an alcoholic, and idiotically made fun of Krill being short. Krill was mature and book smart, but without Rike to stand between them Krill would've castrated Jirkir. Adria probably would've strangled Jirkir if Rike didn't calm her down.

Now that I think of it Adria's the most mature out of the three, he thought. *She's the only one who doesn't drink all the time or rack anybody who makes her mad- wait a minute.* Something caught his eye. Rike saw a large statue of an Arachnid holding a small length of chain. There were a few words on the statue: **Ca yan Jiktre, nur om ri wasop dequefe**.

What's that mean? Rike thought. *Better call Krill on that,* he thought, pulling out his cell phone.

"Hello?" answered Krill.

"Hey, Krill, it's Rike, I need you to translate something."

"Okay shoot," said Krill.

"Uh, 'Ca yan jiktre, nur om ri wasop dequefe,' probably some ancient Arachnid dialect."

"Yeah, I read about that," Krill said, "It means 'to our leader, may he be bound forever.'"

"Okay," Rike said, "and that means?"

"Well, that might have to do with the Arachnid Chain of Leadership. There was this supposed curse put on every arachnid leader involving a small bit of chain," Krill said. "The leaders were said to be bound by that chain to do whatever was in the best interests of their people."

"Huh," Rike said, "didn't seem like Akkrawn did what was in the Arachnid's best interests." "Yeah, I never did figure that out," Krill said.

"Okay, I'll call you if I need anything else," Rike said.

"Alright then, bye," Krill said. Rike put away his cell phone and continued to stare at the statue.

Just then he heard a loud boom and then quickly turned around. A house he had just searched imploded and crumbled. He then heard a cracking sound and then a swift, small, crash. He turned back around to see that the statue had crumbled from the force of the previous crash.

Where the statue had been was an enormous opening that revealed a staircase. *This ground webbing is pretty thick, I guess there are lower levels to Alknarav,* Rike thought.

At the bottom of the steps, there was a vast system of tunnels. Rike also noticed that there were random switches attached to the ceiling.

What he saw next was even more startling. At a point where Rike could estimate was directly below the destroyed building, he noticed that there was a switch there that had been flipped.

Detonators, he thought. *This one was turned on just a few minutes ago, but by who- or what? No one's lived here for the past 384 years.*

As Rike continued down the eerie tunnels, he began to feel a sense of paranoia. He knew he was being watched and followed, just not from where, or by what.
Suddenly, he heard a noise that almost made him pass out. "AAAUUAHAHHHHH! NO! NO! NOOOOOOOOOOO!"

He didn't think about where he was going. He just started running. The screaming grew fainter and louder randomly, which made Rike's situation even more confusing.

As if that didn't scare Rike enough, a few minutes later, the lights in the tunnels shut off. He began to run faster, despite that he was constantly ramming into walls and falling. He could also feel small tremors from the mysterious something detonating bombs.

Finally, salvation came when Rike saw a light in the distance. He ran toward it frantically, and when he reached its source, he was in a large room that looked like some sort of lab. Rike didn't really notice that, however. All he saw was the ladder that led back up to the surface.

He headed toward it, but he was interrupted. "NOOOOOO!" he heard just before he was tackled. He quickly pushed away the assailant. He realized that it appeared to be an arachnid corpse that had attacked him. "NO! NO! NOOOO!" it screamed as it lunged at Rike again. The creature missed him by about an inch, and that gave Rike an opportunity. He grabbed two of the arachnid's arms and forced its head into a nearby tub of green liquid in an attempt to drown it.

What he did apparently worked. The corpse struggled for a few seconds until it flashed green, and then it was gone. He caught his breath and looked at the label on the tub: Removal Formula. *What did it remove, I wonder?* Rike thought as he began observing the lab. There was a single desk in the whole lab. He was even more shocked when he noticed what was on the desk: a test tube filled with a black powder surrounded by a small length of chain.

Needless to say, Rike took the tube and the chain. He looked around the room for anything else that could help him find out what the Temple of Thought was, but all he found was evidence of how gruesomely cruel Akkrawn was to his own people. There were multiple medical tables with stains of blood still on them, there was a chute labeled 'Bodies,' and the room was filled with whips and shackles.

Rike hurried his final sweep of the lab, as he was still a bit shaken from his fight with the corpse. As he neared the ladder, Rike gave the room one last, horrified look. *You know,* he thought as he climbed the ladder, *I hope Akkrawn suffered as much as his people did.*

The North Road Gang

Chapter 7

Miners first started digging the Hillgregg Mines in 1844. The mines had a vast amount of diamonds, but they had all been mined and collected by 1877. However, the mines were never sealed off officially.

Soon afterwards, the Legion began to use the abandoned mines for bases and drug trades. By the 1970s, multiple gangs were using the location for smuggling and other crimes. Jirkir risked his life going there in search of information on the mysterious Temple of Thought.

There was a large mine shaft that led down to the main mines. The second Jirkir got inside, he began to feel cut off from the rest of the world, and the feeling didn't wear off as he was lowered deeper into the ground.

This wasn't the first time Jirkir had gone down into the mines.

"I dare you to go down there," Jirkir remembered.

"Mom and Dad are going to kill us if they find out," said Jirkir.

The North Road Gang

"Mom and Dad don't have to know. Just go down there, look around a little, and then come back up." "Okay," Jirkir sighed. He went down into the mines, and started to wander around. It wasn't long before he ran into two thugs. "What are you doing down here?" said one of them. "You shouldn't be here. Get out, or we'll shoot."

"Hold on, a minute," said one of them. "This kid could be with the Legion. We can't risk him finding out anything." "You're right," said the other one, cocking his gun.

All of the sudden, a hand came out of nowhere and punched the thug in the face. "DAD!" yelled Jirkir.

The elevator door opened. The main chamber was huge and open. It was lit by a bulb so powerful that it would set a room any smaller on fire.

When he got off, Jirkir had a shotgun in his face before he could blink. "You got a mark on ya?" a heavy-looking thug asked him. Marks were distinctive tattoos that gangsters used to tell which gang they were with. "Uh, yeah," Jirkir said. "It's on your gun barrel."

The North Road Gang

The idiot looked right at the gun barrel. Jirkir seized the opportunity and reached for the trigger and pulled. A shot rang out, and the thug was dead before *he* could blink. While Jirkir wasn't very fact-smart, he was one of the slickest fighters in Hillgregg.

Jirkir took the shotgun and ran. He didn't exactly care where he went, as long as he stayed out of sight.

He ran into the nearest sub-chamber, and when he was sure that no one was following him, Jirkir stopped to admire his new shotgun. It was two feet long, made of smooth wood and silver, and loaded with explosive bullets. *Sawed off,* he thought. *Nice.*

"Hey, you!" someone said. "This is North Road territory. Are you a Copperhead?" The North Road and Copperhead gangs were fierce rivals.

Jirkir walked up to the man slowly. "HEY!" he said. "I said, ARE YOU A COPPERHEAD?" Jirkir stopped in front of the man. He quickly shoved the shotgun in his mouth and fired. The gangster dropped to the ground and seconds later, his head exploded. "By the way, no, I'm not a Copperhead," Jirkir said.

The North Road Gang

And Krill thinks I'm such an idiot. I'd like to see him pull that off, Jirkir thought.

Jirkir walked for several minutes before he found something. There was a small hole in the wall of the tunnel just big enough for Jirkir to crawl through. Inside was a narrow path with a strangely flat wall at the end.

Jirkir switched on his telepack's flashlight and shined it on the wall. He was shocked by what he saw. The wall had words carved into it:

The Temple breaths life into the thoughts that venture within its power

What the heck does that mean? Jirkir wondered. He scanned the wall for any other disturbances, but he found none.

He squeezed back out of the opening, and found himself surrounded. At least ten North Roads with guns, clubs, or fists were ready to kill him at any second.

"Take him to Vor," one of them said, " I think he'll want to deal with this one himself."

The North Road Gang

The thugs took Jirkir's shotgun, tied his hands, put a hood over his head, and began leading him down the tunnel.

Jirkir didn't dare speak, as he was sure the North Roads would blow his head off if he so much as breathed too heavily.

Jirkir tripped and stumbled countless times, and the gangsters just laughed at him whenever he did.

They took him to a large room and knelt him down, and, after a few seconds, removed his blindfold.

Before him stood a large, muscular man whose bald head shined so brightly in the well-lit room that it could have been made of steel.
"You must be Vor," Jirkir said sarcastically. The man didn't answer. He just stood their, pointing Jirkir's shotgun in his face.
"Are you from the Crystal Ball Syndicate, trying to take back what used to be your land?" He stood behind Jirkir, still pointing the gun at him. "This is North Road territory," Vor said. "Your body will show everyone that."

Jirkir then realized his feet weren't bound. As Vor was pulling the trigger,

The North Road Gang

Jirkir kicked up and knocked the gun into Vor's face as it fired. Jirkir broke free of his bounds, grabbed his gun and ran.

North Roads were coming at him from every direction. He either pushed them away or shot them. They did manage to rough him up a bit, however. He was covered in cuts and bruises.

When Jirkir reached the exit of the gangs' sub-tunnel, there were four North Roads following him.

He acted instinctively. Jirkir aimed his gun at the entryway ceiling, and he fired. The initial gunshot did nothing, but, as Jirkir hoped, the bullet exploded and caused the entire entrance to collapse.

Jirkir stopped, bent down, and took a deep breath. But his moment of peace didn't last long. Two thugs suddenly approached him.

"Hey," one of them said, "that looks a lot like Larb's gun."

"His name was Larb?" Jirkir said, looking up at them. "Now he seems even stupider!"

This unsurprisingly made the thug angrier, and he punched Jirkir in the face. Jirkir was about to shoot him when he heard a stabbing sound, and the thug fell to the ground.

He quickly looked at the other man, whom he had barely noticed until then. "Um, thanks," Jirkir said.

"No problem," the man said, showing him a badge. "Name's Ecks Mithean, Undergregg Police. You?"

"Is that really that important?," he said, shaking Ecks' hand.

"Yeah," said Ecks, suspiciously, "Why do you ask?"
Jirkir punched him in the face, and ran. He didn't stop until he reached the mine shaft, which he quickly got into, and pressed UP.

Exoskeleton

Chapter 8

The Uppergregg Museum Array was the single largest collection of information in Naxece. Everything that was discovered and noteworthy was there. It wasn't just one museum; it was a whole section of Hillgregg filled with museums on every subject of knowledge.

Krill wasn't new to the museum array, but never in the many times he'd been there had he seen or heard of the Temple of Thought.

"I told you, I'm a friend of Igna's!" he said to the attendant at the museum array gate.

"And I told *you,*" said the attendant annoyingly, "you need a membership card to get in for free."

"I, uh, lost mine," said Krill, recalling the events of the past few hours.

"Then pay the, uh, ENTRY FEE!" argued the attendant.

"Just call Igna, she'll tell you who I am!" snapped Krill.

"This is a complete waste of time," the attendant mumbled as he dialed the phone.

Exoskeleton

"Yeah, boss, some short guy is- okay, I'll let him in."

The man scowled at Krill. "Next time," he said, "you'll just have to pay the entry fee."

"Right," Krill told him, "you keep on believing that."

Igna was the rich owner of the museum array, and, fortunately for Krill, she was a long time friend of his. *And to think,* Krill thought, *just yesterday we were talking about crystal breeding patterns. Today, we'll be discussing something that could mean much, much more.*

Krill headed for the Literary Museum, where he and Igna always went for their talks and discussions.

The Literary Museum was filled with the documentation of every story ever told in the history of Voulkar.

Igna was waiting for him there.

"So," she said, what'll we discuss today?"

"Well," said Krill, "I'm sort of here on unofficial business."

"Oh?" said Igna.

"What can you tell me about something called the Temple of Thought?"

Exoskeleton

Igna's smile turned to a look of shock. "Where did you hear about that?" she asked.

"I read it," Krill answered, "on the war journals of a supposed-to-be dead arachnid general."

"I don't know much about its connection to the arachnids," said Igna, "but I do know something about the Temple itself." Igna looked around to make sure no one was listening. "The Temple of Thought," she whispered, "was a popular legend until the end of the First Millennium."

"So what happened?" said Krill.

"No one knows," said Igna. "The whole story just disappeared from all culture, and only a few people still know about it today."

"So what is it?" asked Krill.

"Even I'm not sure about that," she said disappointedly.

"Then how'd you find out about it?" Krill said.

"I did some digging and a lot of research," she said. "In fact, I know of something in the museum array that might help you."

"What's that?" Krill asked eagerly.

Exoskeleton

"It's in the BioMuseum," she said.
"The BioMuseum?" Krill asked wonderingly.
"Just follow me," said Igna.

Krill and Igna left the Literary Museum and walked through the winding, brick paths of the museum array. They saw many strange museums along the way, including: a museum about the history of doors, a serial killer museum, a junk food museum (very popular among children), and even a museum on the history of museums.

They finally reached the BioMuseum, and it was easy to find, as it was right next to the brightly lit Museum of Neon Lighting.

"It's in here," said Igna, pointing to a room marked 'Extinct Species.'

They entered the Extinct species room was filled with the fossil remains of dead animals, but Igna and Krill ignored them all, and headed straight for a what looked like a large turtle shell.

"This," said Igna, "was the only exoskeleton of the giant grewg ever recovered. It went extinct in 1626-"

"-During the War of the Arachnids," Krill finished.

Krill's cell phone began to ring. "Hang on," he told Igna. "Hello?" answered Krill.

"Hey, Krill, it's Rike, I need you to translate something."

"Okay shoot," said Krill.

"Uh, 'Ca yan jiktre, nur om ri wasop dequefe,' probably some ancient Arachnid dialect."

"Yeah, I read about that," Krill said, "It means 'to our leader, may he be bound forever.'" "Okay," Rike said, "and that means?"

"Well, that might have to do with the Arachnid Chain of Leadership. There was this supposed curse put on every arachnid leader involving a small bit of chain," Krill said. "The leaders were said to be bound by that chain to do whatever was in the best interests of their people."

"Huh," Rike said, "didn't seem like Akkrawn did what was in the Arachnid's best interests." "Yeah, I never did figure that out," Krill said.

"Okay, I'll call you if I need anything else," Rike said.

"Alright then, bye," Krill said.

"What was that about?" asked Igna.

Exoskeleton

"I have a friend who's, um, paying a visit to the Arachnid ruins," Jirkir replied.

"Well, I don't see what that has to do with this, but, anyway," said Igna, "the giant grew was exactly like the modern day grewg, only much larger. Just as friendly, just as clean, just as ideal of a pet."

"So how'd it go extinct?" Krill asked

"Sadly, it's beautiful shell was valued as a decoration and people hunted it until there were only a few left, on a special preserve in Mondas," she said. "It was destroyed when Mondas was."

"Anyway, what's this got to do with the Temple legend?" Krill asked.

"The one bit of information we know on the Temple is that legend says that giant grewg originated from it," Igna said.

"And what tells you that?" Krill asked.

"Some old scroll we dug up from Mondas Battlefield about five years ago," said Igna.

"May I see them?" asked Krill.

"Sure," she said, "they're in the Mondas Museum."

"Where else would they be?" Krill said. During the walk to the Mondas Museum, Krill began to fill with excitement. *Aw,*

Exoskeleton

this is great! I am so gonna rub this in Jirkir's face! He thought.

They reached the Mondas Museum and were immediately transported into an era of great history. A large portrait of the once-great Mondas hung proudly above the main entrance.

"So," Krill said, still half mystified, "where are those scrolls?"

"Oh, right," Igna said, "they're in the archaeology section. Follow me," she said.

The mood in the archaeology section was completely different from that of the main entrance. It was filled with paintings and models of an endless pile of rocks, the remains of a fallen civilization.

"Here they are," Igna said quietly, clearly affected by the room's negative aura.

A small glass case was placed on the wall containing a small, open scroll. It read:

Visper of Mondas, March 3, 1626

Today has never been a finer day to be a man of this fine village. Our towers dwarf all the buildings in Hillgregg, and there is more pride in the air than that in the Arachnid

Exoskeleton

leader's head. My wife and children are as happy as any human can be, as am I. Today we visited the giant grewg, such fine creatures; something so majestic and kind surely must have come from the Temple of Thought. The sun is shining so peacefully, that I feel just warm enough for comfort. Days like this prove that only true happiness can be found here in the fine village of Mondas.

Krill glazed over the words several more times. The words could barely sink in.

"So that's it, huh?" said Krill.

"Uh-huh," Igna said.

Gardenian Labryinth

Chapter 9

The Gardens underwent nearly two hundred years of constant war, until 1546, when the nation's leaders signed a treaty that stated they would renounce all forms of war, and had since been neutral in every war afterwards.

The Gardens were named for their beautiful and various forms of plant life, but were just as well known for the Gardenian Caverns, an intricate system of tunnels and caves that were home to some of the greatest archaeological findings in history, so it was practically common sense that Adria chose the location to look for something related to the Temple of Thought.

Adria walked slowly through the main gardens, just trying to take it all in: the beautifully decorated huts, the exotic plants, and the fruity smell of the place.

"What are you seeking?" someone blurted out.

Adria spun around, and saw there was an elderly man behind her. "Um, uh, what do you mean? I'm just here enjoying the view."

"No, you're not," the old man said.

Gardenian Labryinth

Adria looked disappointed. "What gave me away?" she asked.

"Well, for one thing," the man said with a chuckle, "the first thing you said was 'um, uh.'"

"But how did you know before that?" Adria asked.

"Let's just say, the Gardenian elders know certain things," he said mysteriously. "I am called Certain."

"I'm Adria. Your name is Certain?" Adria asked.

"I said I am *called* Certain," he said. "I did not say it was my name. Now, back to the point, what are you seeking?"

Adria sighed. "The Gardenian Caverns," she admitted.

"You still haven't answered my question," said Certain. "I asked you what you are seeking. You told me where you are seeking to go, but you have still left out what you are actually seeking there."

"You never give up, do you?" joked Adria.

"No, now answer my question," he said.

"Alright," she said. "I was hoping I could find something in there about a Temple of Thought."

"Hmm," said Certain. "In the northwest corner of the Gardenian Caverns, there is a vast, open square, room. "What you seek is at the end of it, but beware of its illusion. That particular chamber is never as it seems."

"I'll keep that in mind," Adria mumbled.

"The Caverns are about a mile north of here. Good luck."

Adria walked away slowly, lost in thought. *So General Carvaner knows where to look too, and hopefully wherever he went still holds value.*

The Gardenian Caverns were deep and somewhat mysterious, but fortunately Adria was too adventurous to worry about that. She walked casually into the entrance, unafraid of what was inside.

Oh, I'm so glad Jirkir's not here, she thought.

Everywhere Adria looked, she saw strange statues and weird symbols carved into the walls. When she finally reached the northwest corner, she began to see strange words written on the walls:

temple of thought

The words were repeated all over.
Suddenly, they were written more
clearly:
TEMPLE OF THOUGHT
Yep, I'm in the right place, Adria thought.
 That was instantly confirmed again
when Adria saw the large room at the
very end of the northwest corner.
Adria stepped into the chamber, and
realized she was standing on a large
platform about an inch above the floor.
"Turn back or die," a voice from nowhere
said.
Adria just stood for a few seconds.
"Your fate is sealed," the voice said.
The door was suddenly sealed shut, and
the platform fell even with the rest of the
room.
Random tiles began to rise up from the
floor into the ceiling, blocking the direct
path to the end of the room.
A labyrinth, Adria thought. *Now there's
a challenge.*
She took a few steps forward, and
suddenly, she felt something was off.
Adria looked down and saw one of the
tiles below he was shaking, and she
immediately jumped off of it. She
moved just in time to see the tile shoot

up into the ceiling, and having been there at the time she would have been crushed.

"Oh, crap," she said, panting.

She got up, but was barely able to stay alive after what happened next.

"DIE!" the voice said.

Adria saw one of the bricks in the maze wall shaking, and she ducked about a fraction of a second before it shot out like a bullet to the other side.

"Gotta do better than that!" she yelled, and continued to work her way through the maze.

"Foolish woman. You'll never defeat me," it said.

"Who the heck are you?"

"I AM THE GARDENIAN LABYRINTH!"

Just the random bricks began shooting out at Adria, and random tiles began violently smashing into the ceiling.

Adria started running, narrowly missing death on numerous instances.

She finally found the end of the maze when she came to a wall with some kind of large cinderblock with a small brick poking out of it. Adria approached it quickly and yanked the brick out of its stone socket.

Gardenian Labryinth

"NO! None have ever passed before!" screeched the Labyrinth in astonishment. "Yeah, well, you've never met me before," Adria said quietly.

The maze fell back into the floor, and the door crumbled, leaving an exit. Adria ran to it, as the room around her was collapsing and caving in.

She jumped out the door just as the exit caved in, and she stopped to catch her breath, and then left the Caverns.

She saw Certain on her way out of the Gardens. "So, how'd it go?" he said with a smile.

"Pretty good," she responded. "I think I killed the Gardenian Labyrinth. Oh, and I got this out of it." She pulled the small brick out of her jacket and showed it to him.

"Hmm," he said examining the object. "This doesn't seem familiar to me in any way, but I can sense that it holds important information."

"I guess I'll just have to find out," she said when Certain gave it back to her.

"Beware," he said, "for an ancient evil has returned to this world. If you and any companions you might have cannot stop it, I fear no one can."

Gardenian Labryinth

"Thanks," Adria said, "I'll keep that in mind."

Galgar's Weaponry

Chapter 10

Jirkir cradled his new shotgun as if it were a newborn baby as the others stared at him in the Ride Chaser. "Good lord," Krill said. "Why don't you just tie the knot and get it over with?"
"Well Krill," Jirkir said, "there's just something about exploding bullets."
"You're an idiot," Krill said.
"Well, at least the rest of us did something that required a little guts!" said Jirkir. "Rike was nearly killed by a killer corpse, Adria was nearly killed by a killer maze, I was nearly killed by killer killers and almost got caught by a cop, and what were you nearly killed by?" he said. "Oh, that's right. NOTHING!"
Krill looked at him for a second. "Still an idiot," he said.
Jirkir sighed. "Come on, guys, back me up-"
"Don't drag us into this!" Adria and Rike said in unison.
Once at Sharp Point Harvesters, they began observing and discussing their findings.
"Okay," Rike said. "I've discovered that the Arachnids were working on some

kind of secret experiment, and they were using their own people as lab rats. I also found this bit of chain, which we can assume is the Arachnid Chain of Leadership that Krill told me about, and I found this test tube next to it, could be just an arachnid's ashes, but it was separated from everything else so I figured it must be important."

Jirkir spoke next. "I saw some strange words carved into a North Road gang tunnel wall. 'The temple breathes life into the thoughts that venture within its power.' What do you guys think that means?"

"To put it in a childish way," Krill said, "I think it literally makes dreams come true somehow. Anyway," he said, "I found that the Temple of Thought is a mostly undiscovered myth, that everybody seemed to forget about after the first millennium. The extinct giant grewg may be connected to the Temple of Thought, and some guy named Visper who lived in Mondas knew something about it."

"I found this in something called the Gardenian Labyrinth," Adria said, taking out the brick.

"Hey, let me see that," Krill said. She handed him the brick, and he threw it on the ground, and it smashed to a pile of dust.

"What are you doing?" she asked.

"The brick's made out of crumine," Krill said. "It's a special type of clay that, when it hardens, becomes extremely brittle. It might have been used to hide something."

He reached into the small pile and pulled out a square piece of wood. "Lo and behold," he said. The wood had writing on it.

f-o

"Interesting," Krill said. "It could mean anything."

"So now that that's established, what do we do now?" said Jirkir.

"I think we should start with Krill's lead, since it's the only on with enough clarity to get us somewhere," Rike said. "We should go to Mondas Battlefield."

"Yeah," Adria said, "but judging from past experience, I think it would be best to be more armed this time."

"Speak no more," Jirkir said. "I know exactly where to go."

"Seriously, Jirkir, where are we going?" Adria asked as Jirkir drove them through Undergregg.

"Oh, you'll see," he said.

"This better not be just an excuse to let you drive," Rike said.

Jirkir turned into an alley and took several more sharp turns before finally stopping in a large junkyard. "What are we going to find here?" asked Krill.

"I heard about this place at the shooting range from some guys who were talking about it," said Jirkir.

"Uh, I'm pretty sure there's no secret about a junkyard," Krill said, looking around.

"You'd be surprised," Jirkir said. "Ah, here it is."

He pointed to a particularly large pile of junk with a door at the front. "Perfectly hidden in a pile of garbage, is Galgar's Weaponry. From what I've heard this place has weapons you can't find anywhere else."

Jirkir opened the door and walked in confidently. The others followed him uneasily.

Galgar's Weaponry

Once inside, they saw a large number of guns and other assorted weapons on racks as far as they could see.

Suddenly, a large man with hulking muscles approached them with a shotgun. "Are you cops?" the man said growly voice.

"No," Jirkir said calmly.

"Oh," he said, tossing the shotgun away. "How may I help you?" he asked in the same growly voice.

"Is this Galgar's Weaponry?" Krill asked.

"No," the man said, scowling at Krill. "What made you think that?"

"Never mind him," Jirkir said. "Anyway, Galgar, we need some decent weapons. We need some that can handle the elements."

Galgar looked at them for a moment. "Hang on a sec," he said, leaving to a different area of the store.

He returned a few minutes later with some boxes. "For numb-nuts," he said looking at Jirkir, "a pair of flame gauntlets. The spikes on them trigger combustion, so anything you hit will catch on fire.

"Thanks," Jirkir said.

Galgar's Weaponry

"Now, for the girl," said Galgar, "a small missile drone. You can pilot it around and shoot little missiles from it."

He turned and looked at Rike. "Here's a scanner gun. You just point it at your surroundings, and it'll identify all nearby living things and structural weaknesses."

His voice became even deeper. "And now for shorty," he said, "a seismium injector. Just stick it in the ground and pull the trigger, and the ground around you will go crazy for a few seconds."

He turned to Jirkir again. "So, numb-nuts, who's paying?"

"Oh, I guess I am," said Jirkir. He gave Galgar the money Plazer had given him. "Will this cover it?" he asked.

"It'll do," Galgar said. Now take your new toys and get out."

They loaded their weapons into the Ride Chaser and drove off. Krill was silent for a while.

"What's the matter, Krill?" Jirkir asked. "Are you shocked that there is, in fact, a seismium weapon, or are you still intimidated?"

"He called me shorty," Krill said.

Chapter 11

Mondas Battlefield was never sealed off to the public, but no one ever had much reason to go there. It was dangerous, as there were many sudden drops and sharp objects, and most items of importance that were to be found there had already been found at some point.

"Come on," Jirkir said as the team trudged through the fallen buildings. "It ain't that bad."

"Hey," Krill said, panting, "what happened to 'My arms! My legs! My whole body?'"

"Give me a break, I was still recovering from a hangover."

They soon came to a large rock that had fallen into a chasm, providing a bridge. Rike was pretty sure, but he decided to use his scanner gun just to be safe.

"Hold on," he said. "This whole thing is weak, if we put one foot on it, we'll fall right into a pit."

"Come on, Rike," said Jirkir. "This is the only way across, but, if you insist," Jirkir said. He picked up a rock, and threw it as hard as he could on to the stone.

The rock broke, but the large stone wasn't even scratched. "Huh," Rike said. "There must be something wrong with the scanner gun."

They began to cross the bridge. "Hey," Krill said, "do you hear that?" He put his ear to the rock. "It sounds like crunching- oh, no," he said. "We've gotta get off this thing, quick. I think it's a-"

Just as he said that, a group of bright orange boarnoits burst out of the surface of the rock. "-boarnoit nest," Krill said. "Run!"

"So," Rike said, trying not to look back at the boarnoits quickly wiggling towards them, "I guess that explains the structural weakness."

"Yeah," said Krill, "They hollow out big rocks like these, and make it so they can get out, but nothing else can get in."

"Krill, at this point, I don't give a crap how it works!" Jirkir yelled.

They reached the end of the bridge, and Jirkir slammed his gauntlets against the rock. It instantly burst into flames, as did the boarnoits. "Well," Jirkir said, "I guess we'll use the jet packs on our way back," Adria said. "Though, you've got to admit, that was pretty exhilarating."

"Yeah, so is a heart attack," said Rike.

They continued on their journey, and as they moved along, they quickly began to notice something. There was a strange noise that sounded almost like a whisper coming from somewhere in the distance. "Okay, that's really starting to scare me," Jirkir said, "If I hear that one more time, I'm gonna start shooting in random directions."

"Please," said Adria, "that'll be another annoyance along with that dumb voice I keep hearing, and that weird whisper too."

Suddenly, a large skeleton jumped out at them, whispering, "You'll pay, you'll pay, you monster, you'll pay."

It lunged at them, pouncing on Krill. Jirkir quickly pulled the corpse away, punching it with his gauntlet. It was burning, but slowly, and it aimed to attack Adria. However, she whipped out her drone and fired a missile at the skeleton. It immediately exploded.

"Whew," Rike said with his hand in his pocket, "that was close."

"What's in your pocket?" Krill asked.
"Oh, it was sort of a just in case thing I brought along," Rike said, quickly pulling hi hand out of his pocket. "Well, now we know the good general did some testing here. That was the same kind of corpse that attacked me back in Alknarav."

"Hey, guys, check this out," Krill said. The others approached a doorway with a sign carved into the wall:

VISPER OF MONADS

CRYSTAL HARVESTING COMPANY

"Huh," Rike said, "our mysterious friend was a crystal harvester."
"Okay, we can marvel at the sign later," said Jirkir, "let's take a look inside."
The building itself was not only intact, but perfectly structurally sound, which was rather strange for a building in Mondas Battlefield. "Well," Krill said, "there's nothing in here out of the ordinary for a 1600s crystal harvester's office. Oh, hey!" Krill exclaimed, holding up a rather bulky-looking backpack. "This was about fifty years before the telepack, so they had to haul all the crystals around." "Yeah," said Jirkir, "while you were admiring that, I found

this," he said, holding up a piece of paper. "To my loving husband," Jirkir read aloud, "maybe this map will help you to not get lost again." Jirkir turned the paper over. "It's a map to Visper's house."

They followed the map to a small, also undamaged residence. They looked around inside, but there was no mention of the Temple of Thought or any sign of anything other than a happy man and his happy family.

That scene changed however, when they entered a small, barely noticeable door that may as well have been part of the wall.

The room beyond that door was a chaotic chamber that looked like it belonged to a psychopath. There was writing all over the walls, and paper with strange writing on it everywhere.

"I think we've found what we're looking for," Jirkir said.

"Hey, guys," Rike said, "I found this note in a readable language."

The Arachnids are coming for me. They're looking for the Temple of Thought. I can only hope that I can finish this last letter before I die, and, that someday, someone may read it. As far as I know the Line that holds the Temple has remained undisturbed by the Arachnids, and they don't even suspect that it's in Hillgregg yet. As I continue to write this, I realize that the life I've lived after straying from the Path has been the happiest time in memory. I think I hear the Arachnids at my door now. They're searching my home, and

"Is that it?" asked Adria.

"Yeah," said Rike, "they must have killed him before he finished writing it."

"Let's go back to the office and figure out where to look next," said Krill.

Suddenly, there was a loud BOOM that shook the entire room. When Rike opened the door, it fell off.

"This must've been some sort of bomb shelter," said Rike. "This could be the result of a motion sensitive bomb, like the ones I saw in Alknarav."

"So, why was it set off now?" asked Adria.

Visper of Mondas

Rike looked at her grimly, and said, "That means Carvaner knew we were here, somehow."

The Transfer of Power

Chapter 12

The group discussed their next move as they sped through the Hillland. "If Carvaner knows we're on to him, we'll have to be really careful about what we do next, to ensure we won't encounter any more surprises," Krill said. "Right now, I think our best bet would be to visit Igna, my friend in the Uppergregg Museum Array."

Just then, the team heard gunfire. Jirkir immediately picked up and cocked his shotgun before anyone could blink. "What the hell was that?" he asked coldly.

"Aw, crap!" said Krill. "We're driving right through the middle of the Hillland Transfer of Power."

"And that is?" Jirkir snapped back.

"Whenever a Hillland ruler dies," Krill explained, "it's a violent tradition that all the parties competing for leadership war out until one party surrenders."

"And how come we didn't know about this?" Jirkir asked angrily.

"They notify every state outside Hillland territories whenever this starts and ends," Krill said, "we must have been in Mondas when it was announced."

"How long do these things usually last?" asked Adria.

Krill looked grim. "Usually a couple days," he said. "The longest Transfer of Power lasted two weeks."

"Well, then we'll just have to hope we make it out alive!" said Rike, slamming on the gas.

The crew made it another ten minutes before Rike came to a sharp turn in the road. He didn't slow down, which was a mistake. The Ride Chaser flew into a ditch, and the team was unable to pull it out.

"Way to go, SPEEDY!" Jirkir yelled at Rike.

"Hey, calm down," Adria said, "and keep your voice down, we don't want to attract any attention from the Hillland troops."

With much protest from Jirkir, the group left the Ride Chaser and walked for several minutes. All of the sudden, they heard a strong, military voice.

"HALT!"

Everyone but Jirkir immediately froze and put their hands up. "Guys, come on, really?" he whispered. "Okay!" Jirkir yelled. "We don't want any trouble, but whoever you are, if you don't let us pass, I will open fire!"

A soldier popped out of a nearby bush and put a sniper rifle in Jirkir's face. "I don't think you want to that," he said. Jirkir put his hands up.

They were taken to a large military base with an insignia painted all over it, clearly representing one of the warring political parties. Inside, there were all kinds of average-looking people, other victims of that army's paranoia.

"Put them in Cell Block D," said one of the soldiers leading them.

They were led into a large room full of bystanders, and the doors shut behind them. "Well, so much for the Temple of Thought," Jirkir said. "Shut up," said Adria, "we've gotten out of worse, we'll get out of this."

"Yeah, sure," said one of the prisoners, "do you even know who our host is?"

"Enlighten me," said Adria.

"His name's Wertuin Clinn," said the man, "he's a fierce competitor for the Hillland Throne. He doesn't take any chances with us 'trespassers.' With luck, we'll live 'till next week."

The Transfer of Power

"I wouldn't count on that," Krill said, smiling. He pulled out his seismium gun. "I told the soldiers this was my medicine, so they didn't take it."

"Stand back!" Rike yelled as Krill poked the seismium gun into the dirt floor. He pulled the trigger, and ran away just as the ground began shaking violently.

The wall split wide open, and a soldier quickly walked in to investigate. Jirkir and Rike ambushed him, and Jirkir stole his gun and shot him.

"Come on," Jirkir said, "let's grab our gear and get out of here."

"Hold on," Adria said, "we can't just leave all these prisoners here."

Jirkir sighed. "Fine," he said, "let's win ourselves a Hillland war."

Taking out the soldiers was easy. Putting a gun in Jirkir's hand made him nearly unstoppable. Half the soldiers were shot, while Rike, Adria, Krill, and some other prisoners beat the other half to death.

After brawling their way through the soldiers, and freeing all the hostages, they were about to leave when several more soldiers armed with bazookas cornered them, and a bulky, muscular man in a decorated military uniform stepped out of a nearby hut.

"I always knew outsiders couldn't be trusted," he said, lighting a cigarette.

"Orders, General Clinn?" shouted a soldier.

"Kill them all," said Clinn, "we can't have any survivors inspiring corruptive bravery in the rest of the Hillland population."

The troops aimed their bazookas, but as they were about to fire, the ground started to shake. The soldiers recklessly began firing in random directions, and they miraculously fired upward and completely missed the crowd. One did, however, fall down and explode next to General Clinn.

"Fall back!" a soldier said. But it was too late. They were already being overpowered and within a minute they were dead.

"Now what?" said Adria.

"Now," said Jirkir, "we find our weapons."

They searched every inch of the prison camp, and finally found a small hut filled with guns and other weapons. The team's weapons were easy to find.

The Transfer of Power

"So now what do we do?" Jirkir asked. "I don't even remember where our car is."
"Jirkir, I think you're going to like this," Rike said. "There appear to be enough army jeeps in this camp for each of us and every one of the hostages."

Each of the team got into a jeep, and Rike got the attention of the other prisoners. "Okay, judging by the maps in this place, Hillgregg should be just a couple hours west. You'll be safe from this war there!" he announced.
"Awesome," Jirkir said, "I've always wanted my own armored jeep, it's a dream come true."

They began to drive away, and as they drove on, Jirkir began to get curious. "Hey, Krill," he shouted, "how'd you get away with shooting that seismium into the ground without getting caught?"
"Simple," Krill said, "I'm short, it was easy to bend over without being noticed."
"Huh," Jirkir said, "a benefit. I never would have guessed it."
"Dear god, everybody stop!" said Krill, getting out of his jeep. "Jirkir come take a look at this."

The Transfer of Power

Jirkir stepped out of his jeep and approached Krill. "What is it?" he asked, looking around. Krill racked him. "Oooh, not there," Jirkir said with a groan.

"You never learn," said Krill.

"Hey, Krill," said Adria, "why do the Hillland people fight these wars?"

"I don't really know," answered Krill, "it could be a 'my army's better than your army' kind of deal, or it could just be another piece of evidence as to the savage instincts of human nature."

"Sorry I asked," said Adria.

Wise Pursuits

Chapter 13

"Look," Krill said to the gate attendant at the Uppergregg Museum Array, "we've been through this before. You know who I am, now let us in!"

"I told you," the attendant said sarcastically, "that you'd have to pay the entry fee this time."

"I'll tell you what you can do with your entry fee," Krill said irritably, "you can take it and SHOVE IT UP YOUR-"

"Maybe I should give those cops a call, who came by earlier, looking for you," said the attendant, with a malevolent smile.

"Here," Rike said, handing the attendant some money. "This should cover all of us."

They walked to Igna's office, a voyage Jirkir could barely stand. "How can you stand this?" he yelled at Krill. "Why would anyone want to visit a fast food museum, or a museum on the history of electrocutions?"

"It's important to somebody," Krill said with a shrug.

They reached Igna's office, and she let the team in, eyeing them suspiciously. "Thanks for seeing me again," Krill said, "I really could use some help with this-"

"Krilden, what the hell have you been doing?" she asked firmly.

Krill hesitated with his answer. "Well, we're still looking for this Temple of Thought."

"Wait, you've been *looking* for it?" she said, in an angry, surprised tone. "That's why I've been getting all kinds of calls and visits from the police, telling me you're now a wanted terrorist?!"

"Well, yeah," Jirkir said, "didn't Krill tell you that the last time he was here?"

Igna only stared at Jirkir with a look that said 'Shut up, now.' She then turned back to Krill. "I thought you were just looking into the subject, not actually trying to find it! And that still doesn't explain why the police paid me a visit, asking me if I'd seen you!"

"Back to what we were here for," Krill said, trying to change the subject, "Adria found something in the Gardenian Labyrinth, and we were wondering if you could tell us what it means. Oh, and we found a weird letter in this Visper guy's house."

Krill handed Igna both objects, and she looked at them intently. "Where did you say you found this again?" Igna asked Adria, holding up the small piece of wood.

"Oh, some living maze in the Gardenian Caverns," said Adria.

"A *living* maze?" said Igna, stunned.

"Yeah," said Adria, it talked, and, oh, it tried to kill me too, but once I took that wood out of its spot, the whole room just sort of died."

Igna stood up. "Did the walls shoot bricks at you and send parts of the walls, ceiling, and floor smashing into you?"

"Yeah," said Adria, getting excited.

"Why?"

"Vivacasary," muttered Igna, quickly leaving into another room, and reappearing shortly with a book. "What you just faced," said Igna, "has its roots in this." The book was titled *Aptwarum.*

"The book of Voulkarian mythology?" said Krill. "This just gets deeper and deeper."

"What your friend Adria just described," said Igna, "was an ancient Aptwarian elder technique known as *vivacasary*. The elders would use it to bring rooms or whole buildings to life to trap thieves or other criminals."

"So, what's that got to do with the Gardens?" asked Adria.

"It's said that some of the ancient techniques are still in use today there," said Igna.

"That would explain why he called himself a 'Gardenian elder.'"

"Who?" said Rike.

"Come on," said Adria, "I'll explain on the way there."

"Hang on," said Igna. "Krill, can I talk to you for a minute?"

"Sure," said Krill. "You guys head on outside, I'll meet you there." He sat down across from Igna. "What is it?" he asked.

"First off," said Igna, "how'd this whole ordeal even start?"

"Well," said Krill, "we were headed for the Silver Towers, we'd just gotten called in to clear out an infestation there."

Igna leaned in closer. "How do the Silver Towers fit into all of this?" she asked flatly.

Krill sighed. "We got there, and the whole place was totaled. Looked like it had been through a war."

Wise Pursuits

"And you never called the police?" said Igna, shocked.

Krill was beginning to feel as if he was in a court of law. "No, I don't recall doing that," he said. "Anyway, we decided to have a look around. I deducted that there was a nuclear explosion that could have originated in a tower near to the Explosives Tower. It was the Genetics Tower."

"What'd you find?" asked Igna.

"We learned that two scientists had secretly brought an Arachnid corpse back to life using crystals."

"That's amazing!" said Igna.

"Back on topic," said Krill, "The cameras showed falsified footage of us blowing up the place."

Krill continued to explain the day's events, from the Arachnid wargraves, to the Transfer of Power, and what brought him to where he currently was.

"Oh my goodness," said Igna.

"I know," said Krill, "a bit hard to stomach, isn't it?"

"Krill, you need to go after wiser pursuits," said Igna.

"What?" said Krill.

Wise Pursuits

"This odyssey you're going on with your friends," said Igna in a concerned tone. "You may think now that you'll get somewhere with this, but believe me, if you keep going, it's not going to turn out good for anyone, especially in a situation like this."

"Maybe," Krill said, getting up, "but I can still try."

"Wait," said Igna. "I suppose you could possibly find the Temple, but I'm not going to let you off on that Silver Towers thing."

"Are you going to turn me in?" Krill asked nervously.

"No," Igna responded. Then she smiled. "In about two hours, I'll call the authorities and tell them you stopped by. I'll say you were looking for the Temple, but nothing else."

"Great," said Krill. "Thanks."

"And Krill," said Igna.

"Yes?" he responded.

"Just try to remember to go for wise pursuits."

"I'll remember that," Krill said.

He left Igna's office to find the others waiting outside. "What was that about?" asked Adria.

"She just wanted to know what was going on. Now, where to next?" asked Krill.

"I know someone in the Gardens," said Adria, "he's the one who led me to the Gardenian Labyrinth."

"Is he this 'Gardenian elder' I heard you mention earlier?"

"Yeah," said Adria, "he's like a living lie detector, his name is Certain."

"Sounds interesting," said Krill.

"Come on," Rike said, "Let's go."

They walked back to their jeeps, but Igna's words continued to haunt Krill the whole way there. *Am I really doing the right thing?* He wondered. Krill didn't mention it to anyone else, especially not Jirkir, whom he knew would hold it against him, but Krill felt a newfound sense of doubt that he couldn't get rid of.

The Equivrian Weapons

Chapter 14

"I think this is where I met him," Adria said, showing everyone in the Gardens where she had spoken with the mysterious Certain.
"You want to know what I think?" Jirkir asked, sneering. "I think-,"
"-that your search is a waste of time?" said Certain, scaring Jirkir so much that he nearly dropped his gun.
"Back again, Adria," exclaimed Certain. "Now, you wanted to question me about the secrets of the Gardenian elders, is that correct?"

The others stared at Certain, cock-eyed.
"I told you," Adria said, "He does that."
"Come with me," said Certain.

They followed Certain deeper into the Gardens. The natural light feeling of the place slowly left the group. The plants got thicker, and the light itself slowly began to disappear. They went through a few dark tunnels, and they came to a small opening in the now Thicket-like Gardens filled with a series of small huts.

The Equivrian Weapons

"Ah, home," said Certain, breathing in the air.

"Savivron!" shouted someone.

"Friend, we are among outsiders, you must speak their language," said Certain.

"Sorry," said the man, turning to Rike, "forgive my stupidity."

"Good day," said Certain, leading the group to his hut.

The hut was filled with trinkets, each one mystifying in nature. To top it all off, there was a strangely dark flame burning in the center. "Now," Certain said, sitting on the floor, "what would you like to know?"

Adria was the first to speak. "What do you know about *vivacasary*?"

Certain's face turned to shock. "Where did you learn the origins of the Gardenian Labyrinth?"

"Come on, old man," Jirkir said, "it was a LIVING MAZE for crying out loud! Did you think we wouldn't look into it?"

Certain frowned at Jirkir for a second, and then sighed. "I was hoping I wouldn't have to reveal this."

He stood up and left the hut, with the others following. They were led to a small hut that had clearly taken some considerable damage. "Oh, no," Certain said, running inside. The group hurried in behind him. The inside of the hut was trashed and there was a bloody body which Certain was kneeling over. "I never knew," he said in a voice that sounded too shocked to be coming from Certain. "I knew arachnids were quick, and, and, stealthy, but, I never could have suspected that the Arachnid could discover what Keep even had, let alone murder him unnoticed."

"Certain," Rike said, "what did your friend have?"

Certain stood up. "You would have called him Keep. He was the only one of us who practiced *vivacasary,* and he knew the location of your Temple of Thought, the only elder entrusted with that knowledge. He never shared it with anyone."

"Let's hope his tongue didn't loosen during his final moments," said Krill.

"Yes," Certain said, "he also held- wait." He began frantically searching around the hut. He opened a drawer, and slowly pulled out a scroll. "Oh, my gosh," mumbled Certain, "he's taken it."

The Equivrian Weapons

Rike approached him. "What did Carvaner take?"

Certain looked at him. "That's his name? Carvaner? Well, Carvaner stole the Equivrian dagger." He handed Rike the scroll. "It's one of three Equivrian weapons."

"Wait a minute," said Krill, "That's impossible. The weapons of Equivrius are nothing but a myth."

Certain turned to him. "You'll find that the line between truth and myth is fuzzier than it appears."

Rike unrolled the scroll. There were a few drawings on it. One was a dagger with a leaf under it, another was a spear with a tree under it, and the other was a club with a right angle beneath it.

"The Equivrian Dagger was here," said Certain, pointing to the dagger. "The Equivrian Spear is kept somewhere in the Trees, and the Equivrian Club is in the Cliffs."

"Of course," said Krill, "a right angle is the universal symbol of the Cliffs."

"Anyway," Rike said, "what's so special about these weapons?"

"They each give a specific power to whoever wields them," said Certain, "the dagger grants incredible speed and agility, the spear grants invulnerability to projectile attack, and the club grants immeasurable brute strength. If all the weapons are held by the same person, it's said that that individual would become the ultimate warrior."

"So, obviously, we can't let Carvaner find all those weapons," said Rike.

"That is," Adria cut in, "if he doesn't already have them all."

"I guess we'll just have to find out," said Jirkir.

"Hold on," Adria said, "we're not leaving yet."

Jirkir sighed. "Why not?" he asked.

"You're still not telling us something," Adria said to Certain. "What do you know about the Temple of Thought?" she asked, losing her patience.

Certain's voice lowered to almost a whisper. "All I know of that cursed place," he said, "is that unimaginable horrors are housed inside of it, and that many have entered it and never left."

"Oh, what a HUGE HELP!" Adria snapped. "Come on, guys, lets get out of here."

They all found their way back into the main Gardens, and Adria seemed to

The Equivrian Weapons

grow more and more furious with each step. "Hey!" Rike shouted, "Why are you being so snippy?"

Adria turned to him. "Because!" she yelled, "every time we follow up a lead on this wild goose chase, we just end up with more problems, and more and more risks! I'm tired of it!"

"Adria," said Rike, "the cops wouldn't believe us if we told them, and we're already in too deep. Carvaner will probably stop at nothing until he's got what he wants in the Temple of Thought, and," he hesitated.

"Until what?" Adria asked.

"Until we're dead," uttered Rike.

There was a long silence as they walked slowly to their jeeps. Krill was the first to break it. "So where do we go now?"

"The Cliffs," Rike said, "we don't have to pass through the hilllands to get there."

"I've said it before, and I'll say it again," snickered Jirkir. "This is insane."

"I think we've established that," said Krill.

Jirkir ignored him. "I mean, how many crystal harvesters get to do any of the things we've done in a single day?"

The Equivrian Weapons

Adria lashed out. *"Get* to do? That's an absolute riot!"

"Calm down," said Rike, "we don't want to do Carvaner's work for him."

"Thanks for reminding me," said Adria sarcastically, relaxing her arm.

Chapter 15

The drive over to the cliffs felt longer to everyone than it actually was. They all felt something coming. Jirkir never let go of his shotgun, and raised it whenever he thought he saw something move. Adria never seemed to close her eyes. Rike kept his eyes fixated on the road. Krill was so alert that he started panting whenever he felt anyone was going too fast.

They arrived after what seemed like days, and stepped slowly out of the car. "Hold on," Rike said, and everyone immediately froze. "Something's not right."

The Cliffs appeared to be deserted. The buildings and structures were apparently undisturbed, but there was no one outside.

"Don't worry," someone said, and Jirkir immediately fired his shotgun. "I haven't wiped them out yet."

They all turned and saw him. He was clearly an arachnid, but there was also clearly something wrong with him. Several parts of his body were filled with crystals, and in one hand, he held the

Equivrian Dagger. This was definitely the murderous general Carvaner.

"So how'd you find us?" Adria asked, clenching her fist.

"You really need to learn to be more careful," said Carvaner. "I left a monitor at that man, Visper's home all those years ago. I retrieved the detonator from the wargraves back in the Thickets."

Jirkir couldn't stand it anymore. He pulled out his shotgun and shot Carvaner. The bullet hit one of his legs, and the bullet exploded, destroying it. But a few seconds later, a new, crystal leg grew back in its place.

Carvaner then continued on as if nothing had happened. "When I was alerted to your presence at that house, I immediately set off the time bomb. After that, I thought I was done with you. However, clearly, I've underestimated you. Now where was I? Ah, yes, now I remember. I ventured to Alknarav to pick up a few things, and they were missing." He turned to them and smiled wickedly. "I believe you have something of mine."

With the Equivrian Dagger on his side, Carvaner quickly leapt at Rike, pinned him down, and searched him until he found what he was looking for: the test tube full of black sand, and the Arachnid Chain of Leadership.

"These will come in handy," said Carvaner, putting the items into his pack. He then sped off in another direction.

"Follow him!" Rike shouted. They all began running trying to figure out where Carvaner had gone.

Krill finally found something. "Hey guys!" he said, "Come here!" Krill was indicating the entrance to a cave with a drawing of a club carved over it, and a sign that read:

PROPERTY OF KEEP
NO TRESPASSING

"Good enough for me," Jirkir said. "Let's go."

The cave was long and winding, but had a lighting system, which made navigation easier.

They eventually came to a large drop in the cave, and Carvaner was on a rock in the middle of it. "A crumine bridge can be useful when you're especially fast, and don't favor followers," said Carvaner. "I'm afraid you've lost," said Carvaner, about to cross another crumine bridge to the other side.

"Not yet!" Rike said. Everyone fired up their jetpacks and chased Carvaner to the other side of the chasm.

They continued the chase throughout the cave, until they came to another chasm. It was a dead end, and people started to panic. "WHERE IS HE?" Rike screamed down the chasm.

"Hold on," said Krill, "I think I know." Krill walked towards the cliff and prepared to jump.

"Krill, NO!" said Rike trying to grab him, but it was too late. Krill had already jumped, and fell down into the darkness.

Adria was ready to cry, when they heard Krill's voice again. "It's okay," he said as some lights flashed on. The 'chasm,' it turned out, had been no more than seven feet deep. "The darkness was an optical illusion," said Krill, smiling. It was made so intruders might never find their way out."

They continued on, and came across more tricks and booby traps along the way. There was a long, narrow stone bridge over a pit full of boarnoits, which they simply flew quickly over. There was a passage similar to the Gardenian Labyrinth, which was longer and seemed more dangerous. Krill solved that problem by injecting seismium in random places every few feet, disabling the trap.

They arrived at a large, open square chamber with an altar holding the Equivrian Club in the center. "There it is!" said Jirkir. They ran to the altar, but when they were about half way there, Carvaner swooped out from behind and grabbed the Club. "I needed to know if it was safe," he said. "The floor began to rumble. "Apparently," Carvaner said, "not any more." He sped out a door in the front leading to a staircase, and the group began to follow him.

Suddenly, a giant part of the floor smashed up into the ceiling. They were barely able to jetpack out of there before the whole room was sealed off.

They walked up the stairs and found themselves behind a house in the Cliffs. Carvaner was standing there. "You really don't know when to give up, do you?" said Carvaner. He sped off quickly.

"Come on," Rike said, "We have to keep going."

As they began to race through the Cliffs, people began to come outside again. They all looked in shock, but were still able to speak. "Is he gone?" someone asked Rike. "I heard that someone saw him leaving the Cliffs." "Crap!" Jirkir said, "We lost him!" "No we didn't," said Rike. "I think I know where he's headed next." "Wait!" one of the Cliff people yelled, "What's going on?" "Nothing," Rike said, "we've got it covered. Just forget everything you've seen." "Yeah," Jirkir said, "just go inside and watch TV, there's probably a game on or something."

They rushed quickly over to their jeeps. "'There's probably a game on or something?'" Adria sneered at Jirkir. "What?" said Jirkir, "Could you think of anything better to say?" "Yeah," Adria said, "you could have said nothing. If people are going to find out what we're up to, we need to look like we have some sort of idea what we're doing."

"So where did Certain say that other Equivrian Weapon was?" Krill asked.
"The Trees," Rike said, "I think he said it was the Equivrian Spear."

"Oh, and Krill," Jirkir said, "Who's Equivrius again?"
"Honestly, when this is over, you are reading the Aptwarum," said Krill. "He was an Aptwarian hero. It's said that his weapons were forged by an elder."
"Yeah, I lost interest after you opened your mouth," Jirkir said as they sped into the hilllands.

The Ultimate Warrior

Chapter 16

They sped through the hilllands, completely ignoring the war surrounding them. They caught up to Carvaner after the first thirty minutes, but nothing they did could harm the monstrous arachnid. Whatever part of his body they shot off, crystal immediately grew back in its place. "Ha!" said Carvaner, "Honestly, I expected a greater resistance than a small group of low-lives wielding toy guns!"

After a great few more insults, they reached the Trees. Carvaner quickly climbed up the Trees. The others headed for the tunnel that led to the upper area, but before they could make it inside, the entrance sealed shut. A voice came over an intercom. "Warning, disturbance detected. All entrances and exits to and from the trees are sealed off until further notice."

"Man!" said Jirkir.

"Don't worry," Rike said, "we'll just take the alternate route." He turned on his jetpack and began rocketing upward.

"Works for me," Jirkir said.

"Sergius Korpin," Carvaner said, cornering the man.

"I swear," said Sergius, "I'm not important."

"Oh, but you are," said Carvaner, "I know Keep entrusted you with the Equivrian Spear, so where are you hiding it?"

"I don't know what you're talking about," Sergius uttered.

A wicked smile formed on Carvaner's face. "Then your purpose is served." He ran one of his crystal arms through Sergius, and he was dead.

Just then, the door slammed open. Carvaner turned around to see Rike and the others standing in the doorway.

"Alas," said Carvaner with a chuckle, "you're too late to save this poor man."

"You've got nowhere to run, Carvaner," said Adria.

"Again, you are mistaken," said Carvaner. He slammed through a closet nearby, and picked up the Equivrian Spear. "I must be going now," he said.

Jirkir once again, attempted to shoot him, but this time the bullet simply shattered to pieces before it touched Carvaner's skin. "That wouldn't have done any good anyway," said Rike.

"Without that spear it probably would have slowed him down," responded Jirkir.

"While you continue your debate," Carvaner said, chuckling, "I'll be making my way to the Temple of Thought."

"No," said Adria pulling out her drone, "You won't."

She fired several missiles at Carvaner, but when the smoke faded, Carvaner remained unchanged.

"I am quick," said Carvaner, "I am strong, and now, with the Equivrian Spear, I am invincible. I am now the ultimate warrior. Now as I was saying, I must be off."

He smashed through a nearby wall and fled into the Trees. The group followed quickly behind him.

As the chase went on, Carvaner began to tease them. "Come on," he said, " a little faster and you just might stop me!"

"Why's he playing with us like that?" Krill said.

"I don't know," said Rike.

"Either way," said Jirkir, "We're gonna win."

The Ultimate Warrior

The Tree people were in a state of mass panic. Everyone was running in random directions, some to observe the chaos, and others fleeing to their homes.

They came to a long, wooden bridge, and Carvaner suddenly stopped in the middle of it. He slipped the Equivrian weapons into his pack.

"Hang on," Jirkir said, "I have an idea."

"This ought to be good," Krill mumbled. They all stood back as Jirkir shot both ends of the bridge with his gun. The bullets exploded, the bridge collapsed, and Carvaner fell through the trees, screaming.

"That was actually pretty smart," Krill admitted.

They began walking back to the entrance to the Trees. "So is that it?" asked Adria. "Is it all over?"

"I guess," Krill said, "but we might as well keep on looking or the Temple of Thought. I mean, that's a lot of historical significance."

"Yeah," Rike said, looking troubled, "I guess so."

"What's wrong, Rike?" said Adria.

"Why did Carvaner stop in the middle of that bridge?" Rike said, "And if he had the Equivrian dagger, why didn't he just use it to sprint away from us?"

"Like I said earlier," Krill said, "He was playing with us."

"Yeah," Rike said, "But why?"

"Maybe he was just crazy," said Jirkir.

"It's possible that he just wanted to show everyone how awesome he was by finding both the Equivrian weapons *and* the Temple of Thought," said Krill, "And when he got to the bridge he decided he'd had his fun and wanted to end on a good note."

"No," Adria said, shaking her head, "Carvaner didn't exactly strike me as a lunatic."

"What did he strike you as?" Rike asked.

"A cold, calculative, narcissistic monster," she said.

"No matter who he was, he's dead now," Jirkir said. "That's all that matters."

Adria laughed a little. "What?" said Jirkir.

"Now, you're starting to sound like a cold, calculative, narcissistic monster," said Adria.

"How does that sound narcissistic?" asked Jirkir.

"Well, you were already that way to begin with," said Adria.

"What bothers me, though," said Rike, is that he made sure the Equivrian weapons were secure, like he knew what we were about to do."

"Then why didn't he just run off?" said Adria.

"It's a bit far-fetched," said Rike, "But I think he might have wanted us to."

"Are you saying he might still be alive?" Krill said in a hushed tone.

"It's possible," Rike said.

"He just wanted a way to get us to stop chasing him," Jirkir said, "And we fell for it."

"I know," Rike said, "But that still doesn't explain why he's strung us along all this time."

"What do you mean?" said Adria.

"When he pounced me back in the Cliffs, he could have killed me right then and there, so why didn't he?"

"Simple," Jirkir said, "He didn't need to. All he wanted was the chain and the black powder, and as far as he was concerned we weren't much of a threat."

Krill turned to Jirkir. "You say that under the impression that people like

Carvaner need a reason to kill," he said. "To him, the only thing that matters is reaching the Temple of Thought. Anything else is just deadweight."

"Which brings me back to my point," Rike said, "why didn't he kill me?"

"Well," Krill said, "the only logical explanation is that he somehow thinks we're important in all this."

"Why would we be important?"

"I don't know," said Krill, "But until we find out, we'll just have to keep looking for the Temple of Thought. Whatever Carvaner wants in there, he's probably closer than ever to getting it."

They reached the edge of the Trees and jet packed down to their jeeps. They noticed something carved into the bark nearby.

Sorry to disappoint you, I'll be in the Temple of Thought.

-Carvaner

"What did I tell you?" said Krill.

"Come on," Rike said nervously, "We've got a lot of work to do."

Jirkir's Flash of Genius

Chapter 17

They rode their jeeps through the streets of Midgregg, trying to decide what to do next. "Should we go back to the Museum Array?" Adria asked.
"No," Krill said, "I don't think Igna will help. Something tells me she doesn't want anything to do with this."
"Then I guess we'll just have to go back to our office and see what we can figure out," said Rike.
"In other words," said Jirkir, "we're screwed."
"Oh, Jirkir, you're such an optimist," said Krill sarcastically.
They arrived at Sharp Point Harvesters and began formulating theories. This, however, turned out not to bring so many results. After a while, they just started throwing out ideas that remotely sounded like they could work.
"Maybe it's at Krill's place," said Jirkir, "He thinks a lot."
"Maybe the Temple of Thought has a mailing address," said Rike, "We could check the post office."
"Or maybe," muttered Adria, "that reference to 'the line that holds the

Temple' in Visper's letter means that the Temple of Thought is actually an attraction that people stand in *line* for."

Jirkir suddenly stood up. "That might be right," he said.

"You're not really helping, Jirkir," said Adria.

"No, not about the theme park thing, but about the line that holds the Temple," said Jirkir.

"How so?" Rike asked, as if just waking up from a fifty-year nap.

"Krill," Jirkir said, "when was the Hillgregg Civil War?"

Krill thought for a second. "In the late 990s, I think," he said.

"Okay, and you said that the Temple of Thought was a popular legend until the end of the first millennium, right?"

"The Fifty-first Parallel," Krill said, "Of course."

"Exactly," Jirkir said, "Whoever knew where it was at the time must have realized that people were getting a little too close, so somehow, they got everybody to stop talking about it."

"It must be in the Undercaves of the Hillgregg Hot Springs!" said Adria.

"Let's head over there," said Rike.

Jirkir's Flash of Genius

"Wait," said Krill, "How are we going to get in there?"

"Oh, there's a way," Jirkir said, smiling. "We can be pretty persuasive when we're holding deadly weapons."

"You know, if we do that, they'll just call the cops on us, and we'll get busted," said Krill.

"Hey," said Adria, "Our goal is tog go into the Temple and stop Carvaner, what happens to us afterwards isn't really important right now."

"Hey guys, why don't we keep talking about the future while Carvaner destroys it?" said Rike. "Let's GO!"

They all hustled into their jeeps, and headed off quickly. They made sure to mind the speed limit. Not that they obeyed it, they just made darn sure they weren't caught breaking it.

Despite their best efforts, Jirkir was caught speeding on one incident just after they entered Midgregg. Everyone except Jirkir saw a police car nearby, and slowed down to below the speed limit.

"Sir, step out of the vehicle, please," said the police officer.

"Sorry officer," said Jirkir, "Me and my friends were just going to see a movie, and the showing's in a few minutes."
"In armed military jeeps?" said the officer. "Seems like an odd vehicle to be driving to a movie in."
"Oh, that?" Jirkir said, pointing to the jeep's turret. "That's, uh, fake," he said.
"Right," said the officer, "I'm jut going to take this jeep to the impound lot, and you can come pick it up after it's been thoroughly investigated."
"Sir, I'm sure we can work something out here," said Jirkir. After he had finished negotiating, Jirkir was riding shot gun in Rike's jeep, and Jirkir's was being towed to the impound lot.
"So what were we going to see?" asked Adria angrily. "Bull Crap: The Movie?"
"Shut up," said Jirkir.
"You know, Jirkir," said Krill, "when you figure out the location of the Temple, I thought you might actually be smart, and then you pulled that back there."
"I guess even I have my moments," said Jirkir.

They soon reached the Hot Springs, and quickly approached the gatekeeper. "Oh," he said, giving them a disgusted look, "I see you're back. What do you want now?"

"We need to get into the Undercaves," Rike said.

"Oh, well, let me just check the list." The gatekeeper looked at his list then gave them a sarcastic smile. "It appears you don't have clearance," he said. "Sorry."

They all pulled out their weapons. "How about now, asshole?" said Rike.

The gatekeeper's sarcasm turned to fear. "G-g-go on in," he said.

"Thanks," Rike said, "we really appreciate it."

They ran in, and Krill quickly glanced back at the gatekeeper. "He's calling the cops," he said.

"So?" Adria said, "Screw him."

When they got to the doors to the Undercaves, they saw that the doors were smashed open. "Well," said Jirkir, "We know Carvaner's been here already."

"Come on," said Rike, "We probably don't have much time."

They ran into the room, and saw that the elevator was still intact. "Why didn't he cut us off here?" said Rike.

"He probably wants us to follow him," said Krill, "so it's probably a trap."

Jirkir's Flash of Genius

"Oh, come on, we can handle whatever he's got," said Adria, "Now let's head down there, we wouldn't want to keep the good general waiting, now, would we?"

They shuffled into the elevator. As the doors closed, they all felt like they were not only descending into the Undercaves, but that they were leaving their world, and entering into another one.

The elevator doors opened, and they immediately saw where Carvaner had smashed into walls, trying to find an entrance to the Temple of Thought. They all began frantically searching for any weak spot in the walls that might mask the Temple's entrance. Jirkir was pulling loose rocks from their foundations. Krill was injecting seismium in random places. Adria was using her telepack to try and suck away at the wall. Rike was using his scanner gun at everything in sight, trying to locate a weakness.

"This is useless!" Jirkir said after a while, throwing a large rock on the ground. "Carvaner probably led us on a wild goose chase!"

"Hang on, guys," said Adria, "I think I've found something."

She was pointing to the door marked 'under construction' that they'd seen earlier that day. It was completely torn from its hinges, and there was a dark tunnel beyond the doorway. "I think that could be it," said Adria. "Let's go find out," said Rike.

Into The Temple

Chapter 18

The group switched on their flashlights as they ventured deeper and deeper into the tunnel's dark abyss. They found nothing for what seemed like several hours. They finally saw a small, flickering light in the distance. They ran up to it, and when they reached it, they realized it was a large, brightly lit, circular room. There were a few burning torches, but the actual source of the room's brightness was undeterminable. "Yep," said Rike, "This is the place."

"Yeah," said Adria, "the only question is, where do we go now?"

A gargoyle statue in the room suddenly spoke. "Only the wise may enter the hallowed halls of The Temple of Thought," it said. "Once I start my journey, there's no going back, my path can be seen in red, blue, or black. What am I?"

"What's it talking about?" Jirkir whispered.

"A pen," Krill said to the gargoyle.

"Good," said the gargoyle, "you and your companions may enter, but beware, for I am only the beginning."

Into The Temple

The gargoyle suddenly became inanimate again, and an opening in the wall appeared, leading to a staircase. "How'd you figure that out?" asked Jirkir. "Simple," Krill said, "the journey is the pen's writing which is permanent, hence the 'no going back.' The pen's path is also the writing, and pens often use red, blue, or black ink."
"What did the gargoyle mean, by 'I am only the beginning'?"
"I hope I'm wrong," said Krill, "but I think he meant that he's not the worst we'll face in the Temple of Thought."

They descended the staircase, and came to a room overlooking a pit filled with a dense fog, and a set of stairs leading to a doorway at the other end. "Adria," Rike said, fire your drone at the ceiling, so we can see how deep that pit is."

Adria shot a missile at the ceiling. A large chunk fell off, but it turned to dust in mid-air, and the missing part quickly grew back. "Crap," she said.

Rike used his scanner gun. "It's about ten feet deep," he said, "and it's structurally sound. There's nothing there but that fog."

Into The Temple

They tried their jetpacks, but they didn't work. "Why won't our jet packs start?" said Adria.
"I think the Temple wants us to cross," said Rike.
"Well, you never know until you give it a try," said Jirkir.
They carefully climbed in, and immediately realized how little they could see in there. "Guys?" called Rike, "you there?"
"Yeah," Jirkir said, "I-ow!" someone punched Jirkir in the stomach. "Krill, what'd I do this time?"
"I didn't-ouch!" said Krill.
"Guys, I think there's something in this fog," Rike said.
As they shuffled through the pit, trying to find the other end, the fog relentlessly continued to beat them.
"Jirkir," Rike finally said, panting, "Use your flame gauntlets. The light may clear up the fog for at most, a few seconds. Hopefully that'll give us enough time to find the other end and get out."
Struggling, Jirkir punched the floor, and it burst into flames, clearing the fog. "Run!" Rike said.

Into The Temple

They ran towards the exit, trying not to get burned by the growing fire. They made it out of the pit just as the floor regenerated. They looked at each other and realized they were all covered in bruises. "I hope we don't have to do that on the way out," Krill said.

"I don't think we do," Adria said. The fog was gone, and the pit rose up until there was a flat path to the other side.

"Well, I've got a good feeling about the next room," said Jirkir.

"Why?" Rike asked.

"I can see it."

They walked down the short hallway, and came to a small room with nothing in it but a door to the exit.

"Let's just get this over with," said Jirkir.

They started walking through the room, but soon noticed that they weren't getting any closer to the other end.

"What's going on?" Adria said.

"Let's stop walking for a second," said Krill, "See what happens."

They stopped right away, and the small room extended into a long hallway.

"It looks like every step we take seems to somehow make the distance longer," said Krill.

"Do you think we could make it to the other side if our feet didn't touch the ground?" said Rike.

"We might be able to use our jet packs," said Krill.

Sure enough, they jet packed over to the other end in a matter of seconds, and when they looked back, the room was small again. "Thank God, they worked that time," said Jirkir.

They entered what looked like an elevator shaft, with a platform extending into it. They could see an exit way down at the bottom. "This is impossible," said Krill, "there's no way to get down there."

The platform suddenly dropped a few feet, and another platform appeared next to and slightly below it. They were walking onto it when the first platform started crumbling to dust. "This is bad," said Jirkir.

Another platform appeared next to that one, and the original crumbled as they were getting on to the next. Adria almost fell, but she got back onto the platform before it crumbled when the next one appeared.

They continued to jump from platform to platform, trying not to stay on any one for too long. When they finally reached the bottom, a staircase back to the top extended out from the wall. "I hate this place," said Jirkir.

They walked down a short hallway into another circular room with a large diamond suspended in the air in the center. Jirkir stopped the others before they went in. "I'll handle it," he said. "Okay," said Rike, "but no 'we're rich' crap."

Jirkir approached the diamond and observed it for a moment. When he finally worked up the nerve to touch it, it fell to the ground and somehow lodged itself in the floor. Jirkir stood back as the diamond began to glow brightly. "Was that supposed to happen?" he said when he rejoined the group.
"Hopefully," Krill said, "otherwise you may have killed us all."
"I hate you," Jirkir said.
"I know," said Krill with a slight smile.

The diamond grew brighter, and it began to flash multiple times. When it had stopped, a doorway appeared at the end of the room.

The group carefully entered the next room, and saw Carvaner. "Oh, good," he said, "It's so nice to see you alive."

Death to the Fearful

Chapter 19

"Welcome to the central hub of the Temple's power," said Carvaner.

"Cut the crap," said Rike, "now what do you want with this place?"

"I plan to usher in a great era of prosperity for the arachnids," he said.

"The arachnids are dead," said Krill.

Carvaner laughed. "You have been to Alknarav, have you not?"

"I have," said Rike. "What were you doing to your own people?"

"That is the key," said Carvaner, "you see, Akkrawn became justifiably fixated on stopping death, to create a more perfect, undying race of arachnids. What you saw was the result of our experimenting."

"Experimenting?" said Adria.

"We formulated and tested several theories, most of them just killed the arachnid test subjects."

"That's terrible!" exclaimed Adria.

"It was their duty to be test subjects," said Carvaner, "it was for the greater good."

"But what if they didn't want to?" said Jirkir.

Death to the Fearful

"DEATH to the fearful!" shouted Carvaner, "and life and other rewards to the brave! Those are the words that the great Akkrawn lived by."

"Akkrawn was a monster!" snapped Rike.

"Akkrawn was a REVOLUTIONARY!" declared Carvaner. "Anyway, we finally found a method that worked, but not necessarily in the way we wanted it to."

"That corpse at Alknarav, and the one at Mondas Battlefield," Rike uttered.

"Yes, apparently your actions in those areas disturbed them," said Carvaner, "you see what happened was, we stopped them from dying, but only that. Their bodies deteriorated and rotted to corpses, and they became savage, and could only continuously repeat their last words before receiving the eternal life formula. After I died, I fell on a syringe of the formula. Fortunately for me, the formula didn't have its full effect beause I was already dead, and wasn't turned into a screaming corpse. When those two humans added their crystals to my body, that became the last piece of the puzzle."

"So why are you here?" said Krill.

Death to the Fearful

Carvaner smiled wickedly, as if relishing in his explanations. "You see, that old man Visper came to visit Alknarav some three years before the campaign started, to visit some old friends. However, they had already turned to our side. One evening, while intoxicated, Visper told of an amazing temple that could make one's thoughts become real. Imagine, the ability to harness something as powerful as the mind, and make it into a weapon. Obviously, this was an opportunity Akkrawn simply couldn't pass up. He did some digging and learned of the Temple legend, and how it had nearly been forgotten after your pathetic civil war. His one mistake, however, was becoming obsessed with the idea that it was in Mondas, because that's where Visper was from. We tore Mondas apart, and, well you know the rest. Both my people and I were destroyed, but no matter. I plan to resurrect the arachnids, using the Temple's power, but they need a strong powerful leader to rule over them. What I plan to do in here is to resurrect Akkrawn."

"WHAT?!" Adria shouted in astonishment.

"He was the greatest ruler of all time," said Carvaner, "but the curse of the arachnid Chain of Leadership couldn't see that. He died before the war started, and we kept his ashes in the test tube you found, until we could bring him back after we had taken the Temple of Thought. The single flaw in his judgment was sending us to Mondas and keeping us there. We were all killed before we could find the real location."

"But Akkrawn was killed by Hillgregg soldiers."

Carvaner chuckled. "Oh, no," "that was a double. We needed to make sure that no one suspected our plan, and that Akkrawn's remains stayed intact."

"So what's our role in all this?" said Jirkir.

"You'd managed to follow me all the way to the Cliffs, I figured you were worthy to be the first to die by the great one's hand."

"So you resurrect him, he kills us, you resurrect all the arachnids, then help him take over Naxece," said Jirkir.

"That is mostly correct," said Carvaner, "except, I don't join Akkrawn, I become him."

"Okay, now you've lost me," said Jirkir.

Carvaner smiled, as if relishing in his explanations. "For this to work, Akkrawn needs a living, healthy arachnid body to inhabit. I have volunteered mine. I sought out the Equivrian weapons to ensure that Akkrawn would be all-powerful and unstoppable. Now if you'll excuse me, I have a leader to resurrect."

Carvaner took the ashes of Akkrawn and the arachnid Chain of Leadership from his pack, and then tossed his pack aside. He dumped the ashes on the ground, and lifted the chain into the air. "Ca yan jiktre," he muttered, "nur om ri wasop ac nord!" He threw the chain into the ashes.

"Krill, what's he saying?" asked Rike.

"To our leader," Krill said, "may he be bound no more."

The ashes caught on fire, and the chain burned away. Carvaner jumped into the fire, and his body caught flame. Everything but his eyes and the crystals burned away.

Death to the Fearful

The group stood back as the figure that was Carvaner started to get back up. The new body consisted of fire, crystal, and a pair of menacing eyes.

"Just try to ignore it," Jirkir whispered.

"It's a monstrous, evil arachnid," Adria said, "not a flippin snake."

"I am not evil," said Akkrawn in a cold, dark voice. "I am all that matters. Without me, the world would die a most horribly painful demise. Without my leadership, Naxece would eventually delve into total and complete chaos. Everyone in this pitiful world is like a scared child desperately crying out for order and discipline, and I offered my hand to them. However, they were too stupid to realize what I could have given them, so they killed me. Now, I have a new body, in which I can bring peace to all individuals, whether they want it or not. Death to the fearful, life to the brave."

"No," Jirkir said, "that's not right at all."

"Beastly humans," spat Akkrawn, "you could never understand the greatness I can accomplish as king of Naxece."

"Either way," said Rike, "we're not going to find out, and neither is anyone else, because you're not walking out of this temple alive."

"You are sadly mistaken," said Akkrawn.

"No, you are!" shouted Krill. He had snuck up next to Akkrawn and he injected seismium into the nearest wall. Krill ran away quickly, but the ceiling fell on Akkrawn before it disappeared.

"Let's get out of here," said Rike.

As they were leaving, however, Akkrawn reappeared. "Did you really think you could destroy me that easily?" he said, laughing.

"Aw, crap," said Adria.

"Now, before I restore my great people, you shall face the full extent of my wrath," said Akkrawn.

He approached Carvaner's pack and drew out the Equivrian weapons.

"Who among you is the leader?" Akkrawn asked.

"I am," Rike said righteously.

Akkrawn smiled wickedly. "Then you shall have the honor of dying first."

Rike quietly reached his hand into his pocket. Akkrawn charged at him with the full speed of the Equivrian Dagger, and the full fury of the Equivrian Club.

Death to the Fearful

Akkrawn stopped right in front of Rike and raised the Equivrian Dagger.

Rike closed his eyes. As Akkrawn was about to strike him down, Rike pulled the test tube from his pocket and splashed the removal formula on Akkrawn.

"Wh-wh-wh-what have you done to me?" stuttered Akkrawn, shaking and spasming in pain.

"The body you now inhabit was brought to life partially by your eternal life formula, and I just gave you the removal formula."

"Y-You fools. Not only have you condemned my great arachnids and me, you have sentenced your own race to a h-h-horrible, p-p-p-painful, s-s-s-s-suff-f-f-erring. NOOOOOOOOOOOOOOOOO!" Akkrawn screamed as he vanished, his last word echoing throughout the Temple of Thought.

Rike's Thought

Chapter 20

"Come on," said Rike, "let's really get out of here." But as they were leaving, the Temple began to shake.

"Krill," said Adria worriedly, "did you just inject more seismium into the ground?"

"I'm not doing this," said Krill.

Suddenly, there was a bright flash of light, and they weren't in the Temple of Thought anymore. They were in an immense, open, dimly lit cave, which seemed utterly familiar to Rike. "What's going, on here?" said Rike, trying to determine where he'd seen the cave before.

"I think I may know," Krill said.

"Big shock there," said Jirkir.

"Anyway," said Krill, "The phrase Jirkir found in the Hillgregg Mines said 'The Temple breathes life into the thoughts that venture within its power.' That could mean that one of our thoughts has become real, and it had some kind of trigger, probably when Rike killed Akkrawn."

Rike's Thought

"That would explain why it's my thought," said Rike, "I'm just not sure which one."

Just then, a loud screech came from deep within the cave. Then the source of that screech revealed itself: It was the giant corpse creature from Rike's dream, only slightly different. It was more vivid this time. Horrific mixes of bone and rotting flesh were twisted into one, hideous, thirty-foot tall form. Boarnoits crawled out of the corpses and oozed out of the beast's mouth.

"Krill," Adria said, panicking, "How do we get out of this?"

"Well, right now I think our best bet is to kill that thing," said Krill.

They all started firing their weapons at the creature, but they had no effect. "On second thought, RUN!!" Krill shouted.

They ran for what seemed like a mile, until they came to a large cliff overlooking a dark abyss. Adria and Jirkir quickly shot their explosive weapons at the ceiling, and the rocks that fell separated them from the monster.

"That won't hold it for long," said Rike, "we need to think of a plan to get rid of it, and fast."

"Hang on," Krill said, "I think I have an idea."

"At this point, even I'll listen to you," said Jirkir.

"Okay," Krill said, "If I can get close enough to that thing to throw my seismium gun down its mouth, you guys can shoot at it to ignite the seismium. That might be enough to rip that monster apart."

"Krill, that's suicide!" said Adria.

"I know," Krill said, "but it's the only way."

"Okay," Rike said with some hesitation, "Let's do it."

Not a moment to soon, the creature broke through the rock wall and started to charge towards the group. Krill ran up to it, and the monster snatched him up. When it roared in his face, Krill swiftly tossed his seismium gun in its mouth. Then the boarnoits approached him, but he was okay. The doubt inside him was gone. He knew he'd done the right thing as the boarnoits ate him alive, and the monster chomped up his body.

Rike's Thought

"NOW!" yelled Rike.

Jirkir shot his shotgun and Adria shot her drone at the beast. Sure enough, the creature began to howl in pain.

Then, all of the sudden, the monster exploded, there was another flash of light, and they were back in the Temple of Thought.

Adria immediately started crying, and Rike comforted her. Jirkir just stood silently, not knowing what to say. "Adria," said Rike calmly, "Look."

Giant grewg were coming gracefully out of the walls. "They must have hid," Adria said between sobs, "when Carvaner came in. Oh, Krill would've loved this." She then started crying so hard, that she couldn't even speak.

The giant grewg stopped in front of them, and seemed to bow. "Uh, thanks," Jirkir said quietly. "Okay guys," said Rike, "This time I mean it. Let's really get out of here."

As they walked out of the Temple, more giant grewg came up to them and bowed. The group acknowledged their presence, and occasionally waved a little. "You know what's ironic?" Jirkir said.

Rike's Thought

"What?" Rike asked.

"We did all this, we saved Naxece from the arachnids, and we're most likely going to go to prison for it."

"Yeah," said Rike, still comforting Adria, "I guess that's the price we pay for our terrible crimes."

They continued on, and exited the Temple of Thought back into the dark tunnel through which they had entered. They didn't bother to turn on their flashlights, because they knew exactly where they were going this time.

Eventually, a strange noise caught Rike's attention. "Hey, guys," he said, "Did you hear that?"

"Hear what?" asked Adria, who had finally stopped crying.

"That noise," said Rike, "It sounded like there was someone in here with us."

They decided to switch on their flashlights, and saw five heavy-built men behind them. They immediately jumped the group, and started beating them.

As the group began to become weaker, one of the five left towards the Temple. "Hey!" he eventually shouted, "Call the Reaper, tell him we've found it!"

Rike's Thought

The other four started to drag the group away. Jirkir eventually broke free, and started hitting the thugs with all his strength. "GO!" he shouted to Rike and Adria.

They started running away, trying not to look back. They raced through the Undercaves and encountered a few more thugs along the way, fighting their way through them.

When they finally reached the elevator, they saw that there were two gangsters guarding it. They stopped in front of them. "Okay," said Rike, "Just let us out. We don't want any trouble with you."

"You got trouble when you came down here," one of them said.

"You people here at the Hot Springs really take security way too seriously," said Rike.

One of the men chuckled. "You really think we're Hot Springs security?"

"Well, actually, I thought you were cops," said Rike.

"Oh, now that's just insulting," the other thug said.

"Let us through," Adria said.

"I don't think so."

"Now," she said.

The thugs just started to laugh. Adria then racked one of them. "Let us through," she repeated.

The other man punched her in the face and knocked her down. As he was about to go for Rike, Jirkir suddenly shouted over to him. "Out of the way!"

Rike quickly pulled Adria safely out of harm's way. Jirkir had fought back the other thugs and retrieved his shotgun, and now he used it to shoot both of the guards.
"Come on!" Jirkir yelled.

They hustled into the elevator and shut the doors before any of the other gangsters could catch up to them.
"Well," Jirkir said, "that's not good."
"No," said Rike quietly, "and I have a feeling it's about to get a lot worse."

Back in the Undercaves, the thugs were searching the Temple. "Hey, guys!" one of them shouted, "Come over here, I found something!"

It was a person, lying face down on the ground. "I think he's unconscious," said the thug. Suddenly, the man began to come to.

Rike's Thought

"Back up!" the thug yelled. All the thugs pulled out their guns and pointed them at the man.

"State your name and business," said a thug.

"What's going on?" asked Krill.